Always My Love

Pride, Oregon
Book 14

Jill Sanders

GRAYTON

This is a work of fiction. Names, characters, places, and incidents either are the product of the author's imagination or are used fictitiously, and any resemblance to actual persons, living or dead, business establishments, events or locales is entirely coincidental.

DIGITAL ISBN: 978-1-945100-91-8

PRINT ISBN: 9798871996287

IS Print: 978-1-945100-92-5

Text copyright © 2024 Grayton Press

All rights reserved.

Copyeditor: Erica Ellis–inkdeepediting.com

No part of this book may be reproduced, scanned, or distributed in any printed or electronic form without permission. Please do not participate in or encourage piracy of copyrighted materials in violation of the author's rights. Purchase only authorized editions.

Summary

Secrets, passion, and a chance at love…

Nick thought he could leave the past few years behind by taking a job as a cop in his quiet hometown in Oregon. But he didn't count on meeting Harper, the fiery bartender who has him thinking about things he shouldn't.

Meanwhile, Harper is struggling to make a new start in a small town where everyone knows everyone else's business. She's determined to keep her secrets hidden, but as she spends more time with Nick, she finds herself falling for him despite her reservations.

Can they overcome their pasts and find a future together, or will their secrets tear them apart?

Prologue

Eight-year-old Harper Lee Davis held onto her little sister Hailey Leslie Davis as if her life depended on it. Because it did. Hailey was only six, which meant it was Harper's responsibility to look out for her.

Once more, they were in the back of her mother's old clunker of a car, driving down the road that led, well, Harper didn't know. She was too afraid to look anywhere but at her sister.

When the car swerved again, Hailey let out a low squeal.

"Shush," Harper said softly.

If their mama heard them complain about her driving, Harper doubted she'd be able to hide the marks from her teacher tomorrow. If there was a tomorrow.

The car jerked again, and they heard the gravel spit up under the tires as their mother yanked the wheel and returned the car to the country road. Hopefully it was the road that led to their home.

Harper had never wished so badly to be in the small run-down building as she did now. At least it was safer than a speeding car driven by a madwoman who was high. Again.

Heidi Davis had never been a good mama to Harper or Hailey. She wasn't even a good person. Most of the time she was high on something.

One time, Harper had seen her smelling paint. At first, she thought her mother was going to finally fix up the small shed-like home they lived in. But a few minutes later, she'd started dancing around and trying to chase butterflies that weren't there, and Harper understood what was going on.

Harper had done what she could to stop her mama from doing drugs. She'd used up all the paint on the walls in her and Hailey's bedrooms, but when she got home from school the next day, there was more paint.

She didn't know what all the drugs were her mother took, but over time she learned what happened to her after. Each drug made her act differently.

When their mother drank liquor, she got angry and hit them or yelled and broke things. There wasn't much in the house that wasn't broken.

The paint caused their mama to dance around and act like a kid, which wasn't all that bad.

One kind of drug that she put up her nose or in her arm caused her to just lie around and not move for days. Another kind of drug that she swallowed had caused her to scream at shadows.

Whatever their mother had taken this time before she'd picked them up from school had turned her mean. Which meant Harper had to keep her little sister as quiet as possible. No complaints. No crying. No questions.

When the car finally came to a skidding stop, throwing both of them into the back of the front seat, Harper relaxed.

Their mother jumped out of the car, slammed the door behind her, and marched into their home.

"She's mad this time," Hailey said softly.

"Yeah, we'd best stay clear. How about we walk over to the creek for a while until she falls asleep?" Harper asked.

Hailey nodded, and they quietly got out of the car and headed across the field.

Halfway to the creek, Hailey tugged on her hand. Harper stopped and looked over at her little sister.

Both of the girls took after their mama. They had long dark straight hair. The only real difference was their mama had lost most of her teeth a while back. Now, she only had three teeth on the bottom and two on the top.

Because of this, both of the girls spent extra time each day brushing their own teeth for fear that they'd end up losing all of theirs as well.

"Harp?" Hailey asked.

"Yeah?" Harper glanced back across the field towards the little house.

"Why does she act like that? Why take something that'll make you angry?" Hailey asked.

Harper shrugged. "Don't know. I guess..." She tilted her head and thought about it. "Maybe she doesn't know how it'll make her act."

Hailey thought about it for a moment then said, "I'm hungry."

Harper sighed and nodded. Both of them had missed lunch since there hadn't been any money today. The school had given them each a milk but they hadn't had any breakfast either, so it hadn't sated their hunger.

"Me too," Harper admitted. "Maybe there'll be a few apples left on the tree by the water."

Hailey smiled, and the girls walked faster across the field.

The only thing they had that was worth anything was each other. They certainly didn't have any toys, books, or nice clothes. Half the time they went to school wearing the same clothes all week long. They were given only so many credits at the beginning of the week so they could eat school lunches for free, but when they ran out, they went hungry.

Harper was at the age where she had started to feel shame about it all, while Hailey was still happily oblivious and just enjoyed the few hours away from their mama that she got each day.

One thing was clear in Harper's mind. Whatever happened to them in the future, there was no way anyone would ever separate her from Hailey. She was all Harper had. All that either of them would ever have. Each other.

Nothing and no one could tear them apart. Even their mama.

Chapter One

Harper felt her heart skip when she noticed the two dark-haired police officers step into the restaurant. That happened any time she encountered one of the police officers in town.

She knew the duo very well. Nick Farrow and Tom Reyes were nice men. Social. Kind. But that didn't stop the worry and fear from almost taking over. They were the law, so Harper kept her distance.

Tom glanced around the restaurant and saw his new wife, Kate, who was Nick's sister, wave from a corner booth across the room. He quickly disappeared.

Nick headed straight for her.

The man was one of the best-looking guys in the small town by far. Still, she couldn't afford to do anything about it.

He was a cop and, well, she was a murderer.

She pasted on a smile as he approached the bar and leaned against it.

"What'll you have?" she asked, trying to sound casual.

"Coke," he answered easily. He watched her as she busied herself getting the drink.

There were a handful of police officers that frequented the Golden Oar restaurant, where Harper had gotten a job tending bar the first week that she and Hailey had moved to the small town of Pride, Oregon. But none were as sexy as Nick, who somehow swaggered when he walked, making Harper think of a dozen things that she'd like to do with him. To him.

The man was sex in a uniform. He was not only the hottest man Harper had ever flirted with, but the most dangerous.

Dangerous because of what it could mean to her and Hailey if he or any other cop in town looked too closely at the sisters.

They were as far as they could get from the small Georgia town they'd grown up in. The one they'd run from over six years ago.

They'd told everyone in town that they'd moved into their uncle's place after he left it to them when he died. The story was true, sort of. Hank Davis was really their great-uncle, and he had indeed died five years back. But Hank hadn't left her and Hailey his run-down cabin on the outskirts of the small town. He'd left the place to their mother, his niece.

All it would take was someone looking into them, and their entire world would come crashing down. Again.

Harper had gotten a job behind a bar mixing drinks and serving beers, again, while Hailey had gone to work serving pizzas at the local pizzeria, Baked.

After being in town for over a year, they'd managed to fix up the old cabin a little. At least the roof didn't leak any longer and the fireplace worked well enough to keep them warm through the winter.

Most of their life had been spent in Georgia where the

coldest it got was around fifty degrees. Here in Oregon, just last week it had gotten below twenty. Plus, it snowed and rained. A lot.

If not for the working fireplace in the two-bedroom place, they would have frozen the first month that they moved in.

She set the soft drink down in front of Nick and started to turn away.

"How was your Christmas?" Nick asked as he shifted his tool belt and weapon slightly and sat down.

"Good," she answered, knowing she had to pretend to be normal. "Quiet. Thankfully. I heard you had a wild time catching that woman who broke into the grocery store."

Everyone in the small town knew how Wyatt Auston's crazy ex-fiancée had broken into the store and locked him in the freezer after attacking Hannah, Wyatt's new fiancée, twice. Nick and Aiden had to break through the store's glass door to save Wyatt.

"Hannah did most of the work. By the time we caught up with the woman, she'd run outside and Hannah was sitting on her." Nick smiled.

The man had the sexiest smile. She just couldn't turn away from it and could not help smiling in return.

"I would've paid anything to see that," Harper joked.

She liked Hannah Crawford. To be honest, the little town had a lot of people in it that she liked. It was only the police that she was leery of. Especially Nick.

She could see herself growing too comfortable around him, forgetting that he was the law, and letting her guard down.

Nick leaned on the counter and lowered his voice. Harper had to lean in to hear his next words.

"You didn't hear it from me, but on Christmas day, I

took Hannah and Wyatt down to the station. Harper wanted to make sure that Lisa, Wyatt's crazy ex, got a proper Christmas meal. She took her a massive plate of leftovers, including pie." He shook his head. "It's nice to be back home. One thing is certain, everyone in Pride is nice right down to the core." He leaned back. "How about you? Tired of small-town living yet?"

She shook her head. "No, it's nice. Though it does take some getting used to. Everyone wanting to know everything about you," she admitted.

Nick's eyebrows rose for a second, then he nodded. "Yeah, I've been back in town for a few years. It's hard when they ask me about my time away. Not something I want to open up about, you know, being in the military." He shrugged then turned his head slightly. "Tom over there moved here about two years back. When he first got here, he was a hard nut to crack. Then he started seeing my sister, Kate," he added with a smile.

They both looked over to where the happy couple were snuggling in the booth while they waited for their dinner. Nick turned back towards her.

"Now they both seem happier. Tom especially, since his past is out in the open." He shook his head. "Watching your father murder your brother and mother must have been so hard as a kid. But it made him the man he is today. The man that's making my sister happier too." Nick chatted on happily, unaware of how uncomfortable the conversation was making Harper, who had turned away to pour a few drinks. "He's a damn good cop because of his past. I'm thankful to have him as a brother-in-law."

"What about you?" she asked, needing to keep the conversation away from herself at any cost. "What made you become a cop?"

His eyes darkened and he turned around to scan the room, as if he was looking for some unseen threat. When he turned back to her, the darkness in his eyes was gone and he shrugged, as if trying to pass off the emotions she'd just witnessed.

"This and that." His eyes ran over her. "How is the remodeling project up at your place going?"

She turned away again, a knee-jerk reaction to him knowing about the work she and Hailey were doing.

"It's a small town. Buck at the hardware store mentioned that you and your sister had been in there a lot since moving into town," Nick explained as he leaned on the counter.

She relaxed or at least tried to appear to relax. "It's going." She wiped the countertop since she didn't have any other orders or customers.

He watched her for a moment. "I wasn't going to eat dinner here but..." He sighed. "I guess go ahead and order me up a burger."

"Your usual?" she asked, glancing over her shoulder.

He nodded and then turned as a group of teenagers rushed through the front door of the restaurant. They were being really loud and, after they knocked a chair over, Nick walked over to have a talk with them. He was so quiet, Harper couldn't make out what he said to them, but when he returned to sit at the bar, the group had quieted down.

"You have a way with them," she pointed out.

It wasn't the first time she'd seen him work nor the first time he'd gotten unruly patrons to quiet down. He'd even hauled out a couple of the regular drunks that frequented the bar a few times. He was a good cop. Even if she hated cops.

Nick looked slightly embarrassed at her praise.

"I was a kid once," he said, and took a drink of his soda. "Hell, most people in Pride remember how unruly I was as a teenager." He shrugged.

She wanted to ask him again why he'd become a cop, but she knew all too well that questions flowed both ways. And it didn't seem like he wanted to talk about himself either.

Instead, she kept the conversation light and gossiped about other people in town. They weren't telling each other anything real about themselves, and that was just fine by Harper.

When Nick finished eating and the evening crowd of bar-goers arrived, she felt thankful she'd made it through one more visit from the sexy cop.

He turned to leave but then stopped.

"Hey, I was wondering..." He shifted slightly, and she instantly knew what he was going to ask. You didn't work behind a bar without knowing when a man was getting ready to ask you out.

Her standard list of reasons to reject him started playing in her mind. But then he threw her for a loop and asked, "Do you have a dog?"

"A... dog?" Harper shook her head, trying to make sure she'd heard him correctly.

"Yeah." He leaned on the bar. "You know, a furry four-legged best friend."

She smiled and leaned on the bar, really warming up to him for the first time. "No, do you?"

"I'm thinking of getting one," he answered.

"What kind of dog?"

He shrugged. "The kind with fur. I'm not picky. I don't think I'd want one of those frilly ones that ride in a purse."

She laughed. She couldn't help herself. The image of

Nick carrying a small dog with a big pink bow on its head in a fanny pack around town popped into her mind.

Nick was smiling back at her. Really smiling. She could tell that he too felt relaxed around her for the first time.

"No, you're more of a..." She narrowed her eyes and tilted her head as she thought about what kind of dog person he was. "A Doberman?" She shook her head. "No, German Shepard."

He frowned. "Don't you think that's a little cliché. Me being a cop and all? I want a personal dog, not a work dog."

She nodded and then snapped her fingers. "You can never go wrong with a Labrador retriever."

He smiled. "That's what I was thinking. Lacey and Aaron Stevens's dogs had a litter a while back. I ran into her and she said a couple of the puppies are still up for adoption."

"Sounds like you have it all worked out," she said as one of her regulars walked in the door and headed for the bar area.

"I was wondering, maybe you'd like to go with me tomorrow to pick one out?" Nick asked her.

Somehow, the invite threw her completely off. Her mind drew a blank as to a reason why she shouldn't go with him. Her brain turned to mush and oddly her tongue got twisted. Before her mind could come up with all the reasons why she shouldn't go, her mouth had said "Sure."

"Great, I'll pick you up around ten," Nick said and quickly made his retreat.

She watched him disappear out the front door, glued to the spot, until Franco snapped his fingers in front of her.

"Hello, beer me," Franco said, looking agitated.

Chapter Two

Nick was practically dancing on air as he drove up the hillside overlooking Pride towards Harper and Hailey's uncle's place.

Nick remembered Hank Davis well. The man had died shortly after Nick had left for basic training, apparently from complications of COPD. Most everyone who mentioned Hank Davis talked fondly about the man, who had once owned the tow truck company in town.

Nick remembered that some years back he'd sold his tow truck company to Robbie.

Nick had driven by the man's house a few times in his life. The old cabin sat on the edge of the hillside just after the turn-off to the road to the Jordan and Stevens homes.

The old place had looked like it was falling in on itself the last time he'd seen it. Now, as he parked in front of the home, he was impressed at the improvements the sisters had made so far.

First off, the roof had new shingles and no longer looked like it was caving in. There was a fresh coat of paint on the outside of the house.

He parked beside Harper's older car and headed up the stairs to knock on the front door.

The little cabin had a lot of potential. The porch needed a little work. Several boards under his feet were loose or practically falling apart.

When Harper answered the door, her long dark hair was tied in one of those long sloppy braids she wore often. She had on a pair of old jeans, a sweatshirt, and work boots.

"Hey," she said with a frown. "You're..."

He raised his eyebrows as she looked him over.

"I'm?" he asked when she didn't finish.

She shook her head and took a deep breath. "I'm just not used to seeing you out of uniform."

He smiled. "It's my day off."

She didn't respond and just ran her eyes over him again as if she were trying to figure him out.

He motioned to his Jeep. "Ready? I told Aaron we'd be heading that way."

"Sure." She reached inside and grabbed the large backpack bag that she always carried like a purse and then followed him outside and locked up.

"I really appreciate this," he said as he opened the Jeep door for her. "I've never picked out a dog before." He climbed behind the wheel and added, "I'm sort of scared. I mean, it's a huge commitment."

"I'm sure it'll be easy once you see them."

"I don't know. I mean, what if I get one that grows up to be rude?" He frowned as he pulled out of her driveway.

"Rude?" She chuckled. "Have you ever had a dog?"

He shrugged. "My parents had a few when we were growing up. You?"

She shook her head. "We had a bunch of wild cats that lived

Always My Love

near us. We could never get close to them, except for one. One time Hailey got scratched trying to get too close and the scratch got infected. We both stopped trying to pet them after that."

"How old were you?" he asked, pulling onto the main road.

"Hailey must have been six." She thought about it. "I had to..." She dropped off suddenly and looked out the window.

"You had to...?" he asked.

"We had to clean it out until the infection went away," she finished quickly. He got the impression that she was lying and wanted to change the subject.

"My parents are dog people." He glanced at her briefly. "This is the first place I thought of coming after I left the military. I knew that after all the years of traveling, I had to come home." He pulled into the driveway of the Stevens home.

"This is the longest we've been in one place. I guess the small-town life grows on you," she said. "We thought it wouldn't. You know, everyone knowing everyone else's business."

"Right." He turned off the Jeep and turned towards her. "I like keeping to myself now." He leaned slightly towards her. "There are things in my past the last few years that I don't necessarily want the whole town to know." He saw her eyes change, soften a little. "Something tells me you know what I mean."

She nodded. "Yes." She glanced towards the house. "It's why I bartend. No one really asks their bartender personal questions. They're usually too busy talking about their own problems."

He chuckled. "Cops too."

She smiled and for the first time since he'd met her, she looked fully relaxed around him.

He wasn't stupid. He knew from the moment he'd met her that she was uncomfortable around him because he was a cop. That didn't necessarily mean she was a criminal. Lots of people who had never broken a single law were uncomfortable around cops. He understood that.

There was something about Harper that drew him in and made him want to make her feel comfortable around him. Maybe it was because he felt they had a lot in common, even though they hadn't even broken through their outer shells.

That was why he'd invited her today. He wanted to know more about her without being too pushy. And he really did want her help picking a dog.

"Shall we?" he asked, motioning towards the house.

She nodded and, before he could open her door for her, she was out and waiting for him.

When they stepped up to the front door of the home, they heard barking. Happy barking.

"Yeah, yeah," he heard Aaron say just before he opened the door.

To his and Harper's surprise, two yellow labs sat just inside the door. Normally, when he was greeted by barking dogs at a door, the dogs rushed through the opened door towards him. But these two sat on their butts, tails wagging, watching them.

Dr. Aaron Stevens was Pride's one and only doctor. He ran the local clinic in town and worked part time at the hospital in Edgeview, usually when his patients from Pride were there.

Nick grew up having the man as his doctor and had

even gone to see him a few times since returning. Besides being his doctor, Nick considered him a friend.

He shook Aaron's hand and motioned to Harper. "Have you two met yet?"

"Sure have. How are you Harper?" Aaron asked.

"Good, Dr. Stevens," Harper answered.

Aaron nodded and opened the door. "These two are Danny and Sandy."

"Like in *Grease*?" Harper asked after a beat.

Aaron chuckled. "Yeah, Lilly named them." He rolled his eyes. "The puppies are in the backyard running around. We like to give the parents some time without the little buggers constantly needing attention. Come on back." He motioned and then started walking through the house.

Nick had been to the Stevens house a few times over his lifetime. It was a nice place that Aaron had supposedly spent his first year in Pride remodeling. The place was gorgeous still. He'd had long conversations with Aaron about the work he'd done when he had been remodeling his own home.

In his youth, he had always loved the two-story home and used to tell himself that one day he'd live in it. When he'd found out it was for sale after returning, he'd snatched it up quickly. Now he spent every free day working on it.

So far he didn't have an ounce of regret for leaving his military career behind and following his dreams to return home. It had been time.

The next step in fulfilling his goals was getting a dog. He'd just finished fencing in his backyard a few weeks ago, so he was ready.

They stepped out onto the back deck and saw a half dozen little yellow furballs rushing around the yard. His heart melted.

When one of the puppies tripped over his feet as he rushed towards him to say hi, Nick scooped the little fella up and instantly fell in love.

Puppy kisses were, in his opinion, better than any other kisses he'd ever had.

He laughed and hugged the little thing to his chest while Aaron and Harper talked and gave their attention to the other puppies.

"It looks like you didn't need my help at all," Harper joked. "I think the dog picked you first."

He laughed. "I think you're right," he said, earning another kiss from the dog.

"The hard part is naming the little guy," Aaron joked.

When the puppy settled down in his arms, he glanced up and saw that Harper was holding one of the boy's siblings.

"Looks like I'm not the only one falling in love over here," he joked.

Harper's eyes jerked up to his. For a split second, he saw shock and a little wariness in her eyes. Then the puppy she was holding licked her chin and she smiled.

"I've never owned a dog. I wouldn't know what to do with one." She buried her face into the little dog's fur. "How is it that they smell so good?"

For the next half hour, they enjoyed playing with the puppies. He played with all of the puppies, but he'd already decided to get the first one that had tripped over his feet to rush and love him. It was easy to tell him apart from all his brothers and sisters thanks to the colored collars they had on. This one's collar was blue. He decided that would be a perfect name for the little guy.

When Nick started calling him that as he played with

him, Harper laughed and started calling each one by their collar colors.

By the time he'd worked out the details of taking Blue home, Harper was trying to talk herself out of taking Yellow home.

"I haven't talked to Hailey about getting a dog," she kept saying, but then she'd hug the little dog again. "What would I do with a dog? I'd have to repair the fence in the yard." She frowned and then hugged the dog again. Then she turned to him and sighed. "I hate you for this."

He chuckled. "You don't have to make the decision today. I'm sure Aaron and Lacey will hold Yellow for a few days."

"Sure." Aaron nodded. "So far only Pink and Green have been promised away."

"Ugh!" Harper groaned and then hugged the puppy again. "Screw it. I'll take her," she said firmly. "I've always wanted a dog."

Nick smiled. "I think it goes without saying that Blue is coming home with me."

Aaron laughed and then slapped him on the shoulder. "There was never any doubt of that."

Chapter Three

What in the hell had gotten into her? She owned a puppy. A dog, before long.

"What now?" she asked Nick as they climbed back into his Jeep.

"Now?" He glanced over at the small fur ball she was holding and the one in his own lap. "Now I guess we head into town and get some supplies." He smiled. "I honestly didn't ask you along today to pressure you into getting a dog too."

She chuckled. "The only one who pressured me was her." She picked the dog up and kissed her, earning a tongue bath in return. "See, pure pressure." She laughed.

Nick's chuckle warmed her and made her relax even more around him.

It was almost as if she'd completely forgotten that he was a cop. A stranger. One that she was trying to keep from finding out more about her past.

"Are you really going to call him Blue?" she asked as they drove slowly towards town.

"Sure, it sort of suits him. Don't you think?" he asked as she held both little dogs on her lap so he could drive.

She glanced down at the little dog and realized it really was a perfect name.

"I watched this show once, when I was a kid," she started.

Nick chuckled and she glanced over at him. The sound sure was sexy. A deep rumble that had her insides vibrating.

"I think everyone watched *Blue's Clues* when they were kids," he said, his eyes on the road. She was thankful he didn't see her frown at his reply.

She'd only watched a few moments of the show as she'd been passing by a storefront. She hadn't known the name of it and only that the main character was a cute blue dog.

"Yellow doesn't really seem like a fitting name for your little girl," he said, glancing at her as they pulled into the parking lot at O'Neil's Grocery.

"I guess I'll have to think of a really good name. Maybe one will come to me," she said with a shrug.

O'Neil's had been owned by Patty O'Neil until a few weeks back, when Patty had passed away from cancer and left the store to Wyatt Auston.

Harper had liked Patty. Even though the older woman had tried to get information about hers and Hailey's past, she'd been respectful enough to stop after the first few days of trying.

Then one day, Patty had taken her hand and pulled her aside in the store.

"Girl, I can see that you and your sister are running from darkness," Patty said as she'd glanced up at Harper from her wheelchair. "I want you to know, whatever is chasing the pair of you, you have family and friends here that will defend you until the death. That's the way this town is. Everyone here has run from one form of darkness or another. We've found peace here and not one person here will ever let harm come to one of our own. And child, you and your sister are one of ours now." Patty had squeezed her hand lightly as a tear had slipped from Harper's cheek.

She liked Wyatt and his fiancée, Hannah, just as much. The couple were in the process of moving into their new home up at Hidden Cove. Harper drove through the neighborhood often and dreamed of one day owning one of the homes.

Nick parked his Jeep and turned off the engine. "This might get a little crazy," he said as he took Blue in his arms.

In the end, they decided it was easiest to put both puppies into a cart while they shopped for dog food, toys, dog beds, and other basic supplies.

Thankfully, Nick knew everything the little ones would need and whenever he placed an item in his cart, she grabbed one for Yellow as well.

Harper spent more than she'd expected but figured it was worth it as the puppy snuggled down and fell asleep in her lap on the trip home.

An hour later, after cleaning up the third puddle of pee on the hardwood floor, she seriously questioned her sanity.

Not only was the little girl barking at every shadow, but she was also peeing whenever she got scared or excited.

Thankfully, the first thing the sisters had done when they'd moved into the cabin was rip out all the old carpet. The smell coming from the mildewed carpet was more than either of them could bear. They'd found beautiful hardwood flooring underneath.

Most of the furniture had to be tossed out as well, but

they'd kept a few items in hopes of fixing up or painting them.

The first few paychecks after they'd gotten jobs had been spent on used mattresses, a sofa, and a kitchen table and chairs from the secondhand store in Edgeview.

The longer the sisters stayed in the two-bedroom one-bath cabin, the more it started to feel like a real home, something they'd never had before.

In the past six years, they'd hopped from hotel rooms to small furnished apartments to rooms they rented on a weekly or monthly basis. Once, in Arizona, they even lived in a homeless shelter.

Neither of them had ever bought furniture before or held jobs for more than a few months. Every day that passed by without something bad happening to them caused both of them to be a little more relaxed.

Whenever she or Hailey had time off, they spent it on fixing up the place as best as they could.

So far, they had cleaned, sanded, and stained the hardwood floors in each room. The old tile floors in the kitchen and the shared bathroom had been cleaned and recaulked.

All of the walls had been painted. She had chosen a soft teal green for her room, while Hailey had gone with a darker sky blue, colors that had been on sale at the hardware store.

They had found a soft cream color for the kitchen, dining area, and bathroom walls. Since the walls of the living room had wood paneling on them, they couldn't paint in that room, but they had cleaned the paneling several times and oiled it until it shined like new.

The most money they had spent on the home to date was on the roof and the fireplace. They'd patched the roof

Always My Love

themselves after purchasing shingles that matched at the local hardware store.

Since neither sister had ever dealt with a fireplace before, they'd hired a local man, Parker Clark, to come clean out the flue and reconnect a few of the pipes that had broken loose. Parker had also offered to help patch and repair the wood porch since it needed some serious work. They would do that whenever they could afford it. Until then, they avoided the loose boards.

Even though the rooms were still mostly bare of furniture, the place was feeling more and more like home.

Harper had recently started hanging up pictures that she'd taken of the local scenery on the walls. She loved using the old camera she'd found in her uncle's closet. She'd never imagined being able to own something so nice in her life or that she'd enjoy taking pictures so much. She'd never had a camera before and had to learn how to use the older camera from videos she'd watched on the library's computer or her old cell phone.

Of course, finding film for the camera and learning how to develop it herself had been a big task. But she'd been eager to learn.

Now, she used a small room off the covered carport as her dark room. She'd blown up the best of the images she'd taken and hung them in cheap frames around the house.

Her favorite picture, of a gray crane sitting on the Pride dock at sunset, hung in the living room right next to the fireplace.

Every image that she hung spoke to her in different ways, whether it was a green leaf in the shape of a heart resting on a pile of dead leaves or an image of an old couple holding hands on the beach at sunset.

She loved each one.

Hailey seemed to appreciate her work as well and never complained when Harper hung another picture. She was almost running out of space on the walls in the small cabin.

After Nick had dropped her and the puppy off, she'd tried to get some more work done. She was in the process of sanding and painting a large desk that had been left in the home.

However, the puppy had other ideas and wanted to play or chew on her shoes. When she didn't give the little girl enough attention, she chewed on a stack of magazines, spreading tiny pieces of paper everywhere in the house.

She stopped her work on the desk, figuring her time was better spent cleaning up after the puppy and training her. Dr. Stevens had shown her a few tricks the puppy's parents knew, and Harper was determined to have the little girl follow in their footsteps.

By the time her sister got home from work, the little girl knew how to sit, stay, and lie down. However, they were still having issues with going potty in the house.

She'd temporarily given Yellow a new name that Harper couldn't say in polite company or in public. However, when the little girl curled up and fell asleep in her lap after playing for two straight hours, her heart melted and she once again changed the puppy's name.

"What is that?" Hailey asked, seeing the small mound in her arms.

"This is Lucy," Harper said with a smile.

"Lucy?" Hailey asked. The small dog woke up and, seeing the newcomer, instantly went into full puppy charm mode.

Hailey laughed and took the small thing from Harper's arms and hugged it as Lucy rained kisses over her sister's face.

Always My Love

"Where did you get her?" Hailey asked.

"Dr. Stevens." She wondered if she should tell her sister that she'd gone with Nick or not.

"Why Lucy?" she asked, sitting down on the floor to let the dog rush around. Immediately, Lucy peed on the floor.

"Lucy!" both of them yelled at the same time.

Then Hailey glanced over at her and started laughing. "Because I love Lucy," she said, and rolled her eyes as she rushed to let the little dog outside.

As she watched the little dog run to the grassy area and finish her business, Hailey cleaned up the mess on the hardwood floor.

"I love her," Hailey said, wrapping her arms around her.

"Yeah." Harper sighed. "I figured we deserve a little normality. She's a little normality. Even if we end up cleaning up after her. A lot."

Hailey chuckled and moved over to sit down on the two chairs they had in the backyard so they could enjoy the firepit they'd made to burn all the crap their uncle had left in his house.

"How was work?" Harper asked as she played tug-of-war with Lucy.

"Good." Hailey glanced at her sideways. "I heard a funny rumor today."

"Oh?" Harper asked, glancing over at her sister.

While Harper had allowed her dull brown hair to grow longer, Hailey had chopped hers into a fun short spring style and had added a few streaks to lighten the overall color.

Harper didn't want to put in the effort to maintain any color and barely had enough time to do anything with it other than a messy bun or a loose French braid.

Both of them were around five-foot-five with their mother's dull brown hair. Hailey looked more like their mother than Harper did. Harper's eyes were dark brown while Hailey's were a soft caramel color.

"Yeah," Hailey answered. "The rumor was that you went on a date this morning with Nick the cop?"

Harper's heart did a little skip. "It wasn't a date."

Hailey's eyes narrowed at her. "Then what was it?"

Harper thought for a moment. "I helped him pick a dog."

Hailey glanced down at Lucy. "And ended up getting one in return?"

Harper groaned. "I couldn't help it. She was just too cute." She bent down and picked the little furball up.

Lucy must have still been tired because she curled into a tight ball and fell asleep in her lap.

"She is cute," Hailey said softly. "What are we going to do with her when we're away at work?"

"I bought a kennel." She motioned towards the back door. "I put it in my bedroom for now. Nick says it's best to introduce them to a smaller area at first at night so they can feel comfortable. I figure I can come let her out on my lunch breaks."

"I can as well," Hailey said with a smile. "She won't be in the crate for long with us around."

"Nick says that after she gets used to the house, she won't destroy everything. As long as we train her. Look, I've already taught her a few tricks."

While Harper ran Lucy through the new tricks she'd taught her, Hailey watched and clapped each time the little dog obeyed.

"Nick says..." Harper started, but when Hailey made a strange noise, she glanced over at her sister.

"I don't need to remind you what could happen to us if

he found out anything about our past." Hailey picked up the small dog and held onto her.

"I know." Harper practically growled it. "And it's not our past we have to worry about... just mine."

Hailey shook her head and then reached over to lay her hand over Harper's. "Whatever happens, we're in this together. To the end." The small dog leaned over and placed her paw over their joined hands, causing the sisters to smile. "All three of us," Hailey added.

Harper relaxed back in the chair and sighed. "Yeah, right."

She always verbally agreed whenever Hailey said those words, but in her heart, Harper knew that if it came down to it, she would do everything in her power to protect her sister. After all, she'd been doing just that since the moment she'd been born and especially after that fateful night.

The night Harper had killed.

Chapter Four

It took Blue two weeks and hours and hours of training to stop peeing in the house. By then, Nick had rolled up all of his area rugs and replaced them with pee pads.

About the only other thing the little dog had learned so far was to sit. He wondered if Harper was having better luck with Yellow.

He hadn't seen her since the day they'd picked up the dogs, and he was dying to see her again. Even though they hadn't really talked about anything personal, he felt as if she'd finally started to relax around him.

It was probably the fact that he hadn't been in uniform that day.

He decided to swing by the Golden Oar and grab a burger to go for lunch before heading home to let the dog out.

He parked next to her car in the parking lot and was a little surprised to see her heading out the back doors towards him when he got out of his patrol car.

"Hey," he said, getting her attention.

One minute she was relaxed and the next her entire body was on guard and tense. Her eyes went wide for a split second before locking with his own. Only then did she relax a little.

At least it was an improvement.

"Hey." She smiled at him. "Heading in for lunch?" She pulled her keys out of her purse.

"Yeah, I was going to grab a burger to go and head home to let Blue out. You? Heading home to let Yellow out?"

"Lucy," she said with a smile. "I named her Lucy."

He nodded. "I like it. Who's she named for?"

"*I Love Lucy*," she answered. "How's Blue doing?"

He shrugged and rested his hand on his belt, a move he made often. Usually when he did that, her eyes traveled down towards his gun. This time, though, her eyes remained locked on his face. Another improvement.

"He's stubborn. At least he's somewhat potty trained. Lucy?"

"Fully potty trained. She learns a new trick every day. Yesterday I taught her how to whisper."

"You..." He blinked and then frowned. "Seriously?"

She laughed. "Yes, what about Blue. I'm sure he's picked up a few tricks by now."

"He can sort of sit," he said with a frown. "Okay, one out of four times he'll sit."

Harper tilted her head. "You know what they say, girls are smarter than boys," she teased.

It was the first time she'd really shown him any of her real personality, and it was a total turn-on. Seeing a glimpse of the real Harper was like seeing sunlight for the first time in your life.

"Your smile is truly amazing," he heard himself saying out loud.

Suddenly, her smile was gone, as if his words had caused the spark to be blown out in one single moment.

"I... have to go," she said, looking around. Then, without responding any further, she turned quickly and unlocked her car.

"Hey." He touched her arm lightly, and she jerked away from him. "I'm sorry, I..." he started.

"No, it's okay, I just... have to go." She shook her head as if frustrated and, before he could think of anything else to say, she climbed into her car and drove off.

Feeling bad, he took a moment to regroup before heading inside to order his food.

He knew something had happened in the sisters' past. That much was obvious to everyone in town. But what? He itched to try and find out. The logical part of his mind knew that was crossing a line. The emotional side, however, wanted to kick someone's ass for scaring them so much that they jumped at shadows. And at police officers.

It was clear to everyone that Harper was jumpy around police. Any police. Not just him. It wasn't just a man in a uniform, either. Military, firemen, and coast guard personnel came and went in the restaurant, and Harper acted relaxed with them. But the second a cop walked in, you could see the tension building. She became an ice queen, stiff and scared.

At first he thought she was running from the law. Then he'd gotten to know her and her sister.

Criminals didn't move into a family member's home and get jobs. And it was obvious they were related to Hank. If they were running, they wouldn't want anyone to know who they were.

This led him down the rabbit hole of Harper hiding from an ex. He knew that not all cops were good. If she'd dated a cop who had been abusive, that might account for her reaction.

Going on that theory, he'd steered clear of her for the first few months. After that, he'd started slowly flirting with her until it had sort of become the norm. He still saw fear in her eyes whenever she saw him in uniform, but there was an attraction towards him as well.

The more he was around her, the more he could see that icy shield that surrounded her emotions melt. When he'd seen her with the puppy, he knew he could no longer hide the spark he felt for her.

He could, however, be a little smoother than blurting out that he liked her smile.

Sitting in his yard on a wooden bench he'd built himself, he ate his burger while Blue ran around the yard, sniffing and peeing on everything.

When his dog gave a few happy barks and rushed towards the side gate, Nick glanced over to see Harper's car parked next to his Jeep.

He set the last of his meal down and walked over to greet her. He was happily surprised when she pulled Lucy out of the car.

"I figured they could use a playdate. I can't stay long, but even a few minutes might help." Harper smiled.

He opened the gate wide for them to step through, happy that Blue didn't try to bolt this time. "That's a great idea," he said as she set Lucy down. Instantly, the dogs started playing with one another as if they'd been together all along.

He wanted to ask Harper why she was really there. It was obvious she was trying something different. Maybe his compliment had gotten through to her somehow?

While they watched the brother and sister race around

the yard together for a few minutes, he kept silent. This was her move.

"I'm not used to compliments," she said after a moment.

He lifted his eyebrows slowly. "I would have thought that you would get them all the time in your line of work. I mean, men drinking beer and being served by a beautiful woman such as yourself..."

She chuckled. "I get what you're doing. I didn't at first, but now I do."

This time when his eyebrows rose, it was genuine. "What am I doing?" he asked as he motioned towards the bench.

They walked over and sat down as the dogs continued to race around the yard.

"You're deliberately trying to make me feel comfortable around you. Dressed like that." She motioned to his uniform.

He wanted to disagree but knew that it was at least a small part of it.

"I'd love to hear why you're uncomfortable in the first place, but something tells me anything you said now might not be the whole story." He leaned back and threw his arm over the back of the bench. "Maybe someday soon you'll realize that, whoever hurt you in the past, we're not from the same mold." She remained silent, so he decided to try a different tactic. "Did you know that I was named after my mother's childhood boyfriend and fiancé, who died in the military?" She shook her head. "I never met the man, but he and my dad were best friends growing up here in Pride."

She watched him. "Hailey and I didn't know our father."

He nodded, happy that she'd at least opened up to him that much.

"Both my dad and Nick joined the army together. After I graduated from high school, I didn't know what to do with myself, so I followed in their footsteps." He sighed and turned to enjoy the view as he rattled on about his boring life. One of the reasons he'd bought the home in the first place was that the beach was less than a block away.

The other homes around his were all higher up on the hillside. His sat lower, making the home feel more secluded. Still, there were unobstructed views of the Pacific from the yard and every room facing west .

When Harper continued to be quiet, he rattled on about his mother and his aunt opening the bakery, about his cousin, Brook, and about his sister, Kate, returning to Pride to start her own dance studio.

"It sounds like you had an exciting childhood," she said, sounding a little sad and distant.

He shrugged. "It wasn't without struggles. Being in a town where everyone knows you and your history, well, it can be tough. Still, it beats not knowing anyone at all. There's a huge benefit to having a group of people around you who will stand up for you. Everyone in Pride is like that." He reached down and picked up Lucy when she brushed against his leg. "What about you and Hailey? Did you move around a lot as kids?"

She shook her head. "No, we lived in the same house all our lives. Up until six years ago." He opened his mouth to ask her more, but she stood up suddenly and took Lucy from his arms. "I'd better get her back home and head back to work."

He stood up as well. "Sure. Thanks for stopping by. I'm sure Blue is going to sleep well tonight," he joked.

She stopped walking towards his gate and turned

suddenly. "If you want, we can do this a few times a week. I don't want Lucy to be lonely."

He nodded, figuring he'd take the win. He was afraid he would mess up his chance if he said something, so he and Blue just followed them to the gate and stood by as they climbed back into the car and drove away.

"Well, buddy, I think that went well." He picked up his dog. "Did you like hanging with your sister?"

Blue gave him a happy bark and licked his face.

"I'll take that as a yes." He laughed as he walked back inside to put Blue back in his kennel until he got off work in a few hours.

The rest of his day he thought about Harper and the conversation they'd had. Normally, he wouldn't tell all the juicy details of his childhood to someone to get them to relax around him.

But it must have worked since she was planning to bring Lucy back to his place to play again.

Maybe she'd agree to come in the evening when he was off work so they could have an actual meal together. Should he invite her to dinner?

So many questions ran through his head as he directed traffic after the high school football game that evening.

"How's the new dog doing?" Tom asked him as they waited for the cars to pass them.

"He's doing good. We're going to work on sitting tonight. I think he's finally getting the hang of it."

Tom chuckled. "I overheard Hailey telling Kate that Lucy knows how to sit, lie down, stay, roll over, and shake already."

"Seriously?" He frowned. Why hadn't Harper told him she'd taught her dog to do all that already when Blue was struggling to learn the basics, like how to sit and that he shouldn't pee on the rug.

Tom slapped him on the shoulder. "Maybe you could hire Harper to train Blue."

"That's not a bad idea." He thought it was an excellent excuse to get to see her more. "Kate and Hailey seem to be getting along great," he said, knowing his sister had struggled to find friends outside of their cousin Brook since returning home.

"Yeah, it's nice. Kate really likes having new friends. So much has changed in the past year and a half. Being married is... well, amazing." Tom smiled.

Nick's smile was genuine. He could tell that Tom was a happier guy since marrying his sister. "You're probably just saying that because you're married to my sister. Remember, I grew up with her. I know she can be a pain in the ass sometimes."

Tom shook his head. "Nope, I'm too happy to notice anything wrong. Plus, I'm sure I can be a bigger pain than she ever could. I guess I'm just lucky she decided to put up with my quirks."

Nick chuckled. "Love sickness has sure spread around. Brook and Ryder are just as pathetic as you guys are."

"Hey, don't knock it until you try it. Speaking of which..." He paused as they switched the traffic to the main road for a few cars that had piled up. "Your sister was happily surprised to hear that you finally made a move on Harper."

He frowned and held in a low growl. "Just because you enjoy talking about your love life doesn't mean I like to."

Tom's smile grew. "You and I agreed when we became partners that we were equals. So..." He waved the last car ahead, and then they shifted back to the last remaining few that were leaving the high school parking lot. "Harper? How'd it go? Did you officially have your first date yet?"

"We got the puppies together and did a little shopping for dog things." He shrugged, remembering the lunch break earlier. "Today we watched the dogs play together as we avoided talking about the dark parts of our pasts."

The taillights from the last car disappeared into the darkness. Tom walked over and slapped him on the shoulder again. "Take it from a guy who is happily in bliss. Those were not official dates. Man up, bro." He nudged him again as they walked back towards their patrol car.

With the disappearance of the last car, they were officially off duty. He would drop Tom off at his and his sister's house, then head home himself. He was on call until the following Friday, so it was his week to keep the patrol car at his place.

"This is exactly why I like to keep my love life to myself," he pointed out as he got behind the wheel.

Tom shook his head at him. "Hey, I had to listen to your advice about your sister. Even your threats."

Nick smiled. "The threats are still pending. Hurt my sister and no one would ever find your body."

Tom laughed as Nick pulled out of the parking lot. "Empty threats because the day will never come when I hurt Kate."

Nick rolled his eyes. "Lovesick wimp." He groaned and had Tom laughing again.

Chapter Five

Why had she agreed to work a double shift the weekend of New Year's? Probably because she knew she had no chance of going out on a date.

She'd worked the large New Year's party at the Golden Oar the year before and had made a lot of money.

The fact that it had been over a year since they'd moved into town still shook her. In the past six years, she had never let them stay this long in one place.

But things were different here. Pride was more like home than any other place they'd ever been. Most of the townspeople didn't know their past, but Harper felt comfortable here and, most importantly, safe. At some point, she'd stopped jumping at shadows.

The strongest argument in her head for sticking around town was the fact that Hailey was blooming here. Her little sister was acting almost normal, like they hadn't come from the worst sort of childhood imaginable, and that was enough to keep them here longer.

Still, Harper knew that at the first hint that anyone was

clued in as to what she'd done one incredibly hot summer night in Georgia, they would leave.

Now, as the guests poured into the bar area and the drink order tickets piled up, she wondered if the couple hundred dollars she'd make in tips that night was going to be worth the back and foot aches she was bound to have the following day. Thankfully, she'd planned ahead and had requested the next two days off.

Putting on her best smile, she filled each order quickly, knowing that the place was filled with family and friends of the bosses.

She knew every single guest and, more importantly, she liked them all too.

When she turned to take the next order, she practically spilled the drink when she noticed Nick standing on the other side of the bar. He was wearing a dark suit, and his black hair was slicked back from his face. It was his smile that gave her pause at first. Then she noticed just how truly sexy he looked in the clothes.

Her mouth watered and her tongue felt twisted. She didn't even trust herself to say hi to him and instead chose to nod and smile back.

"Evening," he said, leaning against the bar. "You look busy." He glanced up and down the bar.

She had roughly six people waiting for her to fill their orders. Still not trusting her mouth to function properly, she nodded.

"I'll wait," he said, taking a seat.

She needed to clear the fog from her mind, so she purposely ignored his presence for the next ten minutes until the bar emptied out as everyone shuffled onto the makeshift dance floor in the main dining area.

"What'll you have?" she asked Nick, happy that she at

least got that much out.

"Just a Coke," he answered. "Designated driver for my sister and Tom tonight." He motioned to the couple, who were dancing happily with everyone else.

She filled his order and then, when she noticed that no one else was waiting, she grabbed herself a soda as well.

"I didn't know you were coming tonight," she said, setting down his drink in front of him.

He tilted his head. "I hadn't planned on it, but when Kate asked..." He shrugged. "What about you? Stuck working?"

"Asked for the shift. Last year I made a few hundred for a couple hours." She smiled and leaned on the bar top as she wiggled her ankles and feet behind the bar.

"Your feet must hurt. Didn't you work the lunch shift today too?"

"It's not the first time I've pulled a double shift. Still, yeah, it's my third one in a row. But I do have the next two days off." This time, her cheerfulness was genuine.

"Nice, I have the next three days off. I've been on call for over a week and a half." He took a sip of his drink then said, "We should do something."

Her eyebrows arched up. Was he really asking her out? She'd thought he was asking her out last time, but it had just been to go get the dogs. Was this time different? Deciding to play along, she asked, "What'd you have in mind?"

He tilted his head and thought for a moment. "The weather is supposed to be nice tomorrow. How about an afternoon sail?"

"Sail? As in... sailing in a boat?" She felt her heart skip a beat. She'd never been on a boat before. Actually, her fear of water was like a massive black cloud that loomed over her. She had never learned to swim. Had never had any cause to.

"Sure, my family has a sailboat. I've been taking it out on the water for as long as I can remember. I bought myself a small sailboat the year I moved back." He narrowed his eyes and ran them over her face. "You're afraid of the water. We could do something else?"

"No," she said quickly, feeling stupid. She could do this. She wanted to do this. To break her old fears. Lock them away. Become stronger. "I'd love to go out on the water."

Nick smiled. "The dogs can join us. They'd love it. I want Blue to get comfortable going out on the boat."

Swallowing her fears, she nodded in agreement.

Just then everyone in the other room started shouting the countdown to the New Year.

Everyone cheered as the balloons and streamers were released, and she thought, "Screw it." She grabbed Nick's jacket collar and pulled him across the bar and kissed him.

It wasn't her first kiss but, by God, it was the first one that turned her knees to rubber while her skin sparked and her heartrate spiked.

When she pulled back, their eyes locked, and for a split second she forgot who she was. Who he was. What he was. Instead, she dreamed of a normal life. One where she could allow herself to fall for a man like Nick. To lose herself in his hazel eyes.

Then someone shouted out a drink order, and she blinked those dreams away as reality crashed back into her thoughts.

"Tomorrow, I'll pick you up at one in the afternoon," Nick called out as the bar grew crowded again.

The next time she had a moment to look around, Nick, Kate, and Tom were nowhere to be found.

"Who are you looking for?" Avery Auston asked, leaning on the bar.

Avery was Hailey's age. Her long fiery red hair and perky attitude set her apart from most others in town. Harper hardly ever liked anyone the first time she met them. Avery was different. From the second she'd met her, Harper knew that Avery was the most genuine person she'd ever met. And the most cheerful.

Maybe she liked her so easily because Avery didn't try prying into Harper's past? Whatever the reason, over the past year they had become close friends, something she'd never had before moving to Pride. It had always just been her and Hailey. It was nice having others she could talk to.

"Just making sure that Nick drove Tom and Kate home," she answered. "More wine?"

"Sure, wine me." Avery slid her glass towards Harper. "I saw the three of them leave shortly after you laid that very hot kiss on Nick." Avery wiggled her eyes.

Harper groaned. "You saw that?"

"Yeah, I'm dateless tonight so I didn't have my face smooshed up against anyone else." Harper laughed. "So, how was it?" Avery asked, leaning a little closer over the bar.

Harper filled Avery's wine glass and then leaned her elbow on the bar. "I... just went for it, you know? I mean, he was there, everyone was shouting the countdown. I've never kissed anyone on New Year's like that before. I've always wanted to and... well, he was there."

"I invited Nick to the Christmas Party I went to as a friend," Avery suddenly said, "just so you know. But him and I..." She shook her head vigorously. "I think it's because we grew up together, and I'm Kate's best friend. I can't think of him any other way than brotherly. Just so you know."

Harper smiled. "Thanks, I hadn't even questioned it. I've seen you two together."

"Good. Now that you're not going to scratch my eyes out or anything, tell me how it was."

"Hot," Harper finally admitted. "Very hot." She thought about it a little more. "He invited me and Lucy to go sailing with him tomorrow."

Avery smiled. "Oh, he finally made his move?"

"Finally?" Harper frowned.

"Sure. Come on, you had to notice how much he's been trying. He sure did take his sweet time. I'm glad you said you'll go."

"I've never been sailing," she said, suddenly. "What should I wear?" She looked down at her black pants and Golden Oar uniform top.

Avery tilted her head while she thought.

"Jeans, a light sweater, tennis shoes, and bring a jacket. Even though it's supposed to be nice tomorrow, it is January in Oregon." Then her smile brightened. "It's January." She cheered. "Happy New Year."

"Happy New Year." Harper laughed and took the hug Avery gave her over the bar.

The next day, Harper changed outfits twice. In the end, she chose a pair of blue jeans, a cream sweater, and her tan sneakers. She took her heavy coat along with her and even packed Lucy a few treats for the trip.

She'd purchased a sweater for the dog online, and as she pulled it over Lucy's head, the doorbell rang.

Lucy sprinted out of her hold and ran barking towards the front door.

Harper was going to have to work on her insistent need to bark at the sound.

"Hey," Nick said when she opened the door after she'd gotten Lucy to sit and stay.

"Hi." Harper kept the door open and then bent down to finish sliding on Lucy's sweater.

"Wow, she has clothes and everything," Nick said with a chuckle. "Blue's going naked today."

She smiled. "If I'm cold, she'll be cold."

"She does already have a fur coat on," Nick pointed out.

Harper narrowed her eyes a little as she stood up to grab Lucy's leash. "This is so much more fun."

Nick chuckled. "Lucy seems to enjoy it." He motioned to where her dog was currently chasing her tail and trying to pull the sweater off.

"She'll get used to it." She clicked the leash on Lucy's collar. Suddenly, her dog's attention was on the leash. "I'm working with her on her leash etiquette," she pointed out as Lucy started biting the leash.

"Yeah, Blue needs some work in that area too." Nick stood aside as they walked out the front door.

Harper paused to lock the door, but Lucy kept tugging on her leash, excited to go somewhere.

Finally, Nick took the leash from her so she could lock the door behind them.

"Got everything?" he asked as they walked to his Jeep.

She tapped her bag. "I think so. I brought Lucy some water and treats. I didn't know how long we'd be out there."

He helped her put Lucy into the Jeep and waited until the brother and sister happily greeted one another before answering.

"A few hours should be good for the first trip." He waited until she was settled in her seat and then shut the door behind her and Lucy.

When he got behind the wheel, she was laughing and hugging Blue, who had jumped into her lap while Lucy explored the Jeep.

As they headed towards Pride's docks, they chatted about the dogs, updating each other on new tricks each had learned. When they passed his house, it still surprised her how beautiful the place was.

Of course, every home on the street was simply gorgeous and had beachy small-town charm.

Most homes around Nick's were three or four stories high, but his was more modest with only two stories that she could see. She figured he'd have a basement, since most homes in the area did.

She ached to see what he'd done to the inside of the place. When she'd arrived in town, he'd been working on replacing some of the wood-shingle siding. The new pieces stuck out in color from the old worn wood for the first few months. Now, however, after getting plenty of sun and weather, everything matched perfectly.

The trim around his doors, windows, garage door, and front door was all painted a warm rustic red.

"You've sure fixed up your home nice," she said as he parked at the docks. His home was less than two blocks from the dock, but they parked in the parking lot anyway.

"Yeah, it's come a long way. When I was a kid, there was a family from Poland living there. After they left, the place sat empty and didn't get any attention." He turned off the Jeep. "You and Hailey are doing wonders for the old cabin."

"We're trying. We're not carpenters, but we manage. Still, I think we have enough saved to pay Parker to help us with a few things."

"If you need a hand with something, I know my way around power tools," he offered.

She thought about turning him down, but the possibility of saving a little money and working with Nick excited her.

"Sure, I may hit you up on that." She tried not to sound too excited.

Nick's smile warmed her, but then he lowered his voice. "We're going to have to talk about that kiss."

She swallowed and took a deep breath. "It was New Year's. You were there." She shrugged, trying to sound as casual as she could.

"Harper." Nick stopped her from jumping out of the Jeep. "That might have been the reason you kissed me, but we both know there was more behind it than just a casual New Year's smack on the lips. Wasn't there?"

She felt her entire body start to vibrate from his light touch.

What was she doing? Nick was everything she should be avoiding. If she allowed herself to be attracted to him, to get closer to him, she could jeopardize everything.

"It can't be anything more than that," she said softly. "I... don't think..." She shook her head.

Just then, both dogs let out happy barks and rushed to the front of the Jeep, as if they'd just realized they'd stopped.

Nick tried to rein in Blue, while she gathered Lucy. "We'll finish this later," he said.

She knew he didn't mean it as a threat, but because of who and what she was, and who he was, in her gut she'd taken it as such.

Why had she agreed to spend a few hours locked out on a boat with the man? How in the hell was she going to not slip up when he was so damned sexy and easy to talk to?

Out of all the hell she'd been through in her lifetime, the next few hours were going to be harder than anything she'd experienced before.

Chapter Six

Feeling the salty wind in his face had Nick laughing and feeling more lighthearted than he'd felt in months. The wind had a bite to it, but the sun's rays warmed his skin.

The contradiction of heat and cold made him feel alive, which is how he always felt when he went out on the sailboat.

They watched the beautiful coast of Oregon pass by them slowly as the motor on the sailboat pushed them through the cold choppy waters.

The coastline had changed over the years. There were new homes scattered along the rolling hillsides that surrounded the small town, which only added charm and character to the area.

They passed the lighthouse that marked the outskirts of the town. He had visited it more times than he could count.

After the first few minutes on the water, both dogs settled at Harper's feet on his parents' dog bed, which they kept on board for their dogs.

As the dogs relaxed more, so did Harper. The first few

minutes after they'd left the docks, she'd been frozen with fear. But then he'd started talking to her about all the trips he'd taken on the sailboat. He told her what the name of his parents' sailboat meant.

"The *Queen Anne* was the cruise ship they went on together after my dad returned from the army. Nick, the guy I'm named after, had purchased two tickets to surprise my mother with. But he didn't make it home. My dad returned home with a box of things from Nick and gave it to my mother. The tickets were inside with a note in case Nick died. Nick had planned on proposing to my mother on the cruise. Instead, my parents went on it together. As friends," he added, and he could see Harper relax even more. "The story goes that when they got to the Bahamas, they went scuba diving. My father was a diver for the army and pretty much an expert. My dad and a kid by the name of Ronny Hammond got pulled out to sea. It took a couple days to find them."

"How horrible," Harper said.

"My father claims it was nothing, but by the time some illegal fishermen hauled them in and dropped them off back on the island, he and Ronny had made national news. Ronny still visits my family every now and then with his own wife and kids. I had a crush on his daughter Faith for a few years in high school," he admitted with a chuckle.

"Oh?" Harper smiled.

"She's married now with a kid of her own." He shrugged. "Still, if not for that trip, my parents claim they wouldn't have gotten together."

"I guess everything worked out for the best," she said.

"Would you like to steer?" he asked, motioning to the wheel.

She frowned and shook her head quickly. "I... no, I don't know how to."

"It's not hard. Like driving. You turn the wheel the direction you want to go. It's not like there's anything out here to hit," he said with a smile.

She glanced around and then scooted towards him. He helped her stand up and then held onto her hips while she gripped the wheel.

"See, you're a natural," he said as she took control.

"You're teasing me," she said over her shoulder.

"Never," he whispered next to her ear.

Her soft scent mixed with the salty air was intoxicating. His hands balled on her hips as he tried to focus on anything other than how wonderfully soft she felt next to him.

That kiss she'd given him the night before had rocked him more than any other had in the past. Not only had it been unexpected, but it had also been stronger than he'd imagined it would be. Sure, he'd been thinking about kissing her. What it would be like. How she would taste. But he could tell by her reaction whenever she'd seen him in his uniform that there was no way she was ready for him to make his move.

Her making the first move had been the sweetest thing that could have happened.

Leaning in, he asked, "So, what makes you hesitate to make another move on me?"

She jerked in his arms, then relaxed, and chuckled. "Make a move? Seriously?"

"Isn't that what the kiss last night was?" He smiled down at her.

She shrugged. "It was just a kiss."

"No, Harper, it wasn't." He turned her slightly until she

was facing him, trapped in the circle of his arms as he held onto the wheel. "Maybe it started out as just a kiss, but it certainly didn't end up like that."

He waited as her eyes ran over his. Then he felt her entire body relax again. "Yeah," she admitted. "I told you, I can't—"

He swooped in and laid his mouth over hers before she could talk herself, and him, into not letting it happen again.

The moment their lips touched—fire, sparks, heat. He felt such a great response from her that his head spun.

"Nick," she sighed as he pulled away. Her hands were balled up in his jacket, holding him close to her. "I... my life is complicated."

"Whose isn't?" he said, holding onto her. He felt his arms vibrate as he told himself to go slow.

"I... I can't." She rested her forehead against his chest. "There's just too much at stake. You wouldn't understand."

"Then help me understand. Talk to me," he suggested as she moved over to sit down again.

He shut off the small engine and let the boat coast, then sat next to her.

She frowned. "Are we... is this safe?"

He chuckled. "Again, there's not a lot we can run into out here." He took her hand in his. "Whatever is in your past, share with me or don't. It doesn't matter," he said, meaning it. "I think we both know there's something between us." He waited a heartbeat.

"Yes," she finally admitted with a sigh. "Damn it," she groaned, causing him to smile. "Why couldn't you just... I don't know, have bad breath or kiss like a fish?"

He chuckled. "Sorry."

She rolled her eyes. "Okay, so what now?"

He arched his eyebrows as he thought. "Now, we see

Always My Love

where this goes. Enjoy where the current takes us." He leaned back and wrapped his arm around her shoulders. "Then, when you're ready to share what's behind you, we dive in and handle it." He took her hand in his. "Together."

She frowned as she looked down at their joined fingers. "You're very trusting."

"You forget, we've known each other for over a year." He pulled her closer to his chest. "And I like the way your breath smells and the way you kiss too."

She chuckled and then groaned as both dogs tried to jump up on their laps.

"How about something to snack on before we head back?" he asked after the dogs were once again settled on the bed.

While he pulled out the cooler he'd filled with grapes, cheese, crackers, and soft drinks, she had the dogs do tricks to earn treats. By the time he'd finished setting up the small table, Blue was sitting and lying down every time Harper asked him.

"How do you do that?" he asked, completely amazed. His dog obeyed her better than he did him.

"He knows you're a softy. You probably give him a treat even when he doesn't do what you ask of him." She scooted down to the table area.

"Yeah," he admitted. "He looks at me with those big eyes and I melt."

She chuckled. "Softy. You have to show him who is boss."

"He is," he said, earning another laugh from her. "Okay, so I need to be tougher on him."

"Not tougher, just... stronger against his cuteness." She took a slice of cheese and a cracker.

"What about human food?" he asked as Blue begged. Lucy remained snuggled on the dog bed.

"No, you don't want him to get in that habit." She motioned to his dog, who had his paw on his knee. "Don't get me wrong, some human food is good for them. But only give it to him in his bowl and after you've finished eating. Eggs, rice, chicken, those type of things. I've switched Lucy to an all-natural dog food I get up at Carrie's place. She and Josh came in the other night and told me about it. I can tell Lucy likes it much better than the dry food O'Neil's carries. Wyatt says he's going to start carrying the healthier stuff in the store soon."

He sat back and listened to her talk about Lucy's diet and habits. He wondered if Harper knew that she talked about everyone in town as if they were her family instead of friends.

He knew that she'd had a difficult time feeling relaxed around everyone the first few months she'd lived there. Now, she talked as if she was a local. In truth, she was. He knew that everyone she mentioned thought of her and her sister as family.

Whatever was hiding in her past, every person she'd mentioned would overlook her faults and stick up for her if the chance arose.

"It's getting late. We'd better head back towards town," he said when he saw her shiver as a gust of wind hit the sailboat. He'd let them drift while they ate and talked and happily realized they were heading back towards town already. "Here." He handed her one of the blankets his mother kept onboard for cold days.

She snuggled under it and smiled when both dogs jumped up to cuddle with her as he pointed them back towards home.

"This was more fun than I thought it would be," she said as the lights from Pride appeared in the distance. "I've never been out on a boat before. For some reason I thought it would be... scarier."

"It can be. I've been out on the water during a bad storm. All I could think was that this is how Iian Jordan lost his hearing. And his father."

"Right." She nodded. "When you first asked me, that's all I could think of. I heard that story the first month I worked at the Golden Oar. I've learned a few signs so I can communicate with him, but I'm still rusty."

He smiled. "I took American Sign Language in high school. Most schools don't offer it as a second language, but Pride does."

"I guess having your sister be the mayor of the town pays off," she joked. "Is it strange having your partner be your brother-in-law?" she asked after a moment.

"No, it's nice. Tom and I have gotten along since day one." He could tell she was thinking and waited for her to get out what was on her mind.

"His past... I suppose that's why he decided to become a cop." It was more of a statement than a question.

He nodded. "It played a big part," he agreed.

"Does he talk about it with you? What he went through?" she asked.

He nodded again. "Some."

She looked down at her hands. "We—Hailey and I—didn't have the best childhood."

He held his breath. "I'm sorry to hear that," he said when she didn't continue.

Her eyes moved up to his. "Our mother, she was an addict."

He took a deep breath. There. This was the reason they were afraid of cops.

He knew from experience that many addicts with kids taught them to fear authority, especially the police.

"That must have been hard on you two," he said slowly.

She scanned his face. "We had each other. That's all. I would do anything to protect my sister."

He nodded, understanding the love between siblings. "I feel the same about Kate."

Harper seemed to relax and then smiled. He cut the engine and coasted into his parents' slip and then tied off the sailboat.

"How about we drop these two off at my place and head to Baked for some pizza?" he suggested once he was done securing his parents' sailboat next to his smaller one.

"I'd like that," Harper said, gathering her things.

Chapter Seven

The moment they stepped into Nick's house, her curiosity had her scanning around his place.

The front door opened up into the living room and attached kitchen area. Light hardwood flooring ran throughout the massive space.

The walls were painted a soft gray color and only a few pictures hung on them. The windows had blinds on them but they were currently open to allow the colorful sunset to fill the room.

His furniture was modern and appeared brand new. A dark gray leather sofa sat against a wall of windows and faced two soft gray leather chairs. A huge leather ottoman acted as the coffee table and had a tray on top that held bright yellow flowers in a blue vase.

There was a gas fireplace in the corner between two walls of windows that looked out to the backyard.

Nick hung up his coat and Blue's leash on a wall of hooks next to the door while she took a moment to further explore what she could.

His kitchen was huge. The cupboards had glass fronts

on them and were made from the same light wood as the floors. All of the appliances were stainless steel and appeared to be brand new. Actually, everything she could see appeared new, including the marble countertops. The dining room table and chairs sat on the opposite side of a high-top bar area with four bar stools.

She could make out a coffee bar on the back side of the kitchen just beyond his refrigerator.

"Blue's kennel is back here," he said, motioning for her to follow him through the kitchen.

There was a massive laundry room past a small powder room. Besides his washer and dryer, there was a full freezer and rows and rows of shelves filled with canned goods.

Blue rushed into his kennel and snuggled down, and Lucy happily climbed in with her brother.

"Do you think they'll be okay sharing for a while?" he asked as he shut the door behind the dogs.

"I think they're going to sleep the entire time we're gone," she said. Then her curiosity got the better of her. "How about a tour of your home before we head to get food?"

"Sure. This is the laundry slash storage area for all the canned food my mom and aunt think I need to eat." He smiled. "Plus, I use this as a mud room now that I have Blue. He comes in a little wet and covered in sand when we take walks on the beach. That door leads out to a walkway. Less than a block away is the beach."

She nodded, then followed him out of the room. "The kitchen, dining room, living room."

She smiled. "I saw them quickly. I like your coffee bar area." She ran her hand over the marble countertop.

"I built that. This space used to be just a wall. This door leads to the garage." He motioned to the door next to the coffee bar. "Powder room, which I finished remodeling a few months ago."

She poked her head into the small space.

The walls were painted a pale blue. There was a pedestal sink, a toilet, a small window that she guessed looked out to his side yard, and a painting over the toilet of a sailboat.

"Nice," she said and then followed him back through the kitchen. He opened a solid wood door.

"My pantry." He waved his hand.

She stepped in and gasped. "This is a dream."

There were shelves of organizers all labeled with their contents. A countertop held his toaster, blender, and air fryer. Everything was so organized Harper wanted to take a picture of it so she could recreate it at her place, somehow.

"Thanks, but I can't take all the credit. Blake Stevens came up with the design. Actually, all of my furniture and the colors in the place are her doing," he admitted.

"Wow, she did an amazing job." She followed him down a little hallway.

"We'll head downstairs first." He stood back as she took the stairs at the end of the short hallway, then followed her to the basement.

She hadn't expected to step into a massive music room. Guitars hung on the wall above a grand piano.

"You play?" she asked, walking over to the piano.

"I had lessons while Kate danced. I like the guitar better. It's more manly, or so Kate always joked." He grinned.

"I always wanted to learn," she admitted with a sigh as she looked around the rest of the room. There was a soft tan leather sofa and a small desk area, as well as a glass door that she could tell led out to his garage area.

Since the home sat nestled into a hillside, each floor had access to the outside.

"Through here is my home theater of sorts." He motioned to an archway.

She followed him and stepped into the first space that really felt like Nick. The walls were painted a warm gray and littered with a mishmash of paintings and photographs of his family. A black-and-white photo of Nick's family from when he was a kid hung over the sofa. She gauged that he must have been around sixteen at the time. Kate looked so pretty. The perfect family. Her heart ached and she turned her eyes away to check out the rest of the room.

There was a worn sofa and heavy coffee table covered with remotes and newspapers.

"You spend a lot of time here," she pointed out.

"Here and the music room. There is a guest room on this floor too. I never go in there," he joked, and she walked out of the room to follow him down a short hallway. "It has a full bath, which I do use when I'm down here." He opened the doors.

Sure enough, the guest room was very nicely put together. A queen-sized mattress sat on a very chic white oak frame with matching nightstands and dresser. There were watercolor paintings of the ocean and starfish on the walls.

The room was like something out of a magazine. Pretty and perfect, but sort of untouchable.

The bathroom had doors leading from the bedroom and hallway so you could access it from either direction. The beach theme flowed into this room, but there wasn't as much of it.

A massive tile shower stall took up one of the walls.

"That's nice." She motioned to the shower. It was far bigger than the one she and her sister shared.

She'd never showered in something so nice, so large.

"Yeah, it was a bitch to build though. There was a small tub in here that had seen better days. It was pink." Nick groaned. "My dad and I spent two weeks doing this whole bathroom ourselves."

"Wow." She looked at the room with a renewed interest. If he could do something like this, maybe he could help her fix up her bathroom?

"We can head upstairs," he suggested, and she followed him back up the stairs. "There's a total of four bedrooms and three and a half bathrooms in this place," Nick said as they climbed the stairs that sat off the living room. "I gave Blake Stevens full range to decorate the three guest rooms but took over when it came to my own space."

Each bedroom she poked her head into was just as nice as the one downstairs. The walls in one were a soft sky blue, while the other was a little darker blue, like the sea during a storm. The bathroom that sat between those two was nice but a little bare.

Nick's bedroom and bathroom took up half of the upstairs floor. The moment she walked into it, she could tell that this was his space. He wasn't a clutter type of person, so there weren't dirty clothes or junk lying around. Instead, there were little things she knew he used often. Remotes, phone chargers, a massive dog bed at the foot of the bed.

She chuckled. "I bet you that Blue hasn't spent one night sleeping in that thing." She pointed to the bed.

Nick chuckled. "Nope," he agreed. "He only lays in it when I'm showering."

The bathroom attached to the bedroom was as big as one of the other bedrooms.

Both rooms were painted that soft gray color and had more nautical-scenery paintings hanging on the wall, including an image of his small sailboat, which he'd shown her earlier that day.

Next Stop. That was the name of his sailboat. He'd told her that it was the first thing that had come to his head when naming the sailboat. She liked the name. Always looking for the next adventure.

She supposed that's what her life had been like in the past few years. Even though part of her mind knew she was running, part of it also wondered where her life would take her.

"I really like your place," she said as they headed back down the stairs and out to his Jeep.

"Thanks. As I said earlier, Blake pretty much gets a hundred percent of the credit," Nick said, holding the Jeep door open for her.

"Sounds like you rebuilt a lot yourself," she pointed out when he climbed behind the wheel.

"Sure, manual labor was good for me when I came back into town." He started up the Jeep. "I had some... things to work through."

She frowned. "Things?"

He shrugged and avoided her gaze as he pulled out of his driveway. He glanced sideways at her for a split second. "You have things in your past you hold off sharing. I feel the same way about my time in the army."

"I didn't mean to—" she started, but he stopped her.

"Soon, maybe we'll both open up. For now, I'm starving," he said with a smile, instantly lightening the mood.

"Okay, then your childhood isn't off limits?" she asked.

"Nope, that's the best part of my past." He grinned as

Always My Love

he found a parking spot in front of Baked. "What do you want me to tell you about growing up in Pride?"

She smiled. "Everything."

As they ate their loaded pizza, Nick proceeded to do just that, starting clear back at the first time he remembered going out on the sailboat. He covered his first kiss, to a girl named Kathy, and his first girlfriend, Ava.

"That relationship lasted a whole three months, until I caught her kissing my ex-friend Billy." He narrowed his eyes as if he still held a grudge.

"How old were you?" she asked, feeling very lighthearted.

Nick tilted his head slightly. "Fifteen, I think." He leaned his elbows on the table. "What about you? Surely you had a boyfriend?"

She stilled, and her entire body went tense. "Nope, I've never been in a real relationship before." She tried to keep the lighthearted mood but could tell Nick was taking that information in.

"What about your first kiss?" he asked.

Again, she paused. "Snuffy. He was the cat that scratched Hailey."

Nick chuckled and thankfully moved on with the conversation.

Even though her past was a complication she didn't like to think about, let alone talk about, she loved hearing all about Nick's childhood. The town of Pride somehow felt more hers after hearing about it through the eyes of a man who had grown up in it.

"Look, it's snowing." Nick motioned to the dark windows.

Sure enough, thick white flakes floated slowly down to the ground, highlighted by the light from the streetlamps.

How could she ever imagine leaving a place like this? Still, she knew that if things went south, she'd have to.

Only, this time, Hailey wouldn't be coming with her. Her sister had become just as enchanted with Pride as she was. There was no way she would rip her from something so wonderful. Hailey deserved to live in such a charming place. Harper didn't.

As they drove back to Nick's place, she had pretty much figured out a plan for bugging out and leaving her sister behind if the need arose.

When Nick parked back in his driveway, he turned to her.

"Something in you has changed." He shifted to get a better look at her. "You went to a darker place."

She was a little surprised that he could tell. Even though she'd kept up the light conversation, it was true. Just the thought of having to leave had caused a sadness to almost overwhelm her.

"I like Pride," she said, looking down at her fingers. "The thought of having to leave here makes me sad."

"Leave?" Nick asked. "Why would you have to leave?"

Her eyes moved up to his. "Sometimes your past catches up with you."

They were both silent for a moment. "You're more of a mystery than I thought you'd be. Still, who you are is clearly written in your face and your actions. You're not a bad person, Harper." He reached over and touched a strand of her hair. "Whatever you think is coming for you, if you let me, I'll stand in its way."

"Why would you?" she asked, frowning slightly.

He smiled. "I'd think that was obvious." He pulled her across the console and kissed her.

Chapter Eight

Nick poured everything he felt towards Harper into the kiss. The entire day he'd been thinking of this moment. Remembering the taste and feel of her lips against his.

Whatever darkness was behind her, he wanted to show her there could be light in her future. Her entire body vibrated next to his. Then he made a move to get closer and wacked his knee against the gear shift.

Harper laughed and pulled back.

"The front seat of a Jeep probably isn't the best place for this," Harper suggested.

He wanted to invite her in. Upstairs to his room. But something had him second-guessing himself. Whatever happened between them, he wanted it to mean more than any other relationship he'd had before. There was a drive deep in his gut to make what was between them special.

Maybe it was because she'd admitted to him that she'd never had any sort of relationship before. Or maybe it was simply because he wanted to show her not all police or men are bad.

Whatever the reason, when she pulled back, he decided to give himself some time to cool off.

However, the moment they stepped into his house, she plastered herself up against him and pushed him against the wall.

They could both hear the dogs happily barking, and he knew that both of them would need to be let out soon.

"Harper," he groaned out a warning as his hands moved to her hips to hold her still. She was rubbing her body all over his. "We'd better let the dogs out."

She smiled and then happily stood back. Then she followed him back to his laundry room. The moment he opened the kennel door, both dogs sprung out. Blue headed towards the back door a few feet from the kennel while Lucy rushed to Harper.

"They can go out here," he said. "The yard is fenced."

Once he opened the door, Lucy followed Blue out. Nick flipped on the porch light.

While they watched the dogs rush around in the fresh falling snow, Harper wrapped her arms around him.

"I hadn't planned... I didn't invite you today..." he started.

She reached up on her toes and covered his mouth with her finger before kissing him quickly. "I know you didn't invite me sailing today to get me in your bed. But trust me when I say I want to be there."

"From what you've told me, you don't do casual. Neither do I. Just so we're clear."

Her smile slipped slightly. "I'm okay with that. Just as long as you don't expect me to completely open up to you. There are things I won't..." She shook her head. "I can't ever tell you."

He searched her eyes for a moment. "Just as long as it's

not that you're married"—he smiled—"whatever secrets you have can remain yours."

They stood back as the dogs rushed inside and shook off the fresh layer of snow covering their fur.

"They can stay down here tonight. There's water, food." He motioned to the bowls.

She took his hand in hers and, after shutting the dogs in the laundry room, walked towards the stairs.

He followed her up to his bedroom, afraid that if he said anything he'd break the spell she had him in.

The moment they stood inside his bedroom, she pulled off her coat and set it on the chair in the corner. Then she walked over and pulled off his coat as well.

Their boots were next, but he stopped her when she reached for his sweater.

"Let me," he said, pulling her body up against his and kissing her. "I could lose myself in your kiss," he admitted. "You're the sweetest addiction. I can see myself wanting more and more."

She smiled as she ran her fingers through his hair. Then she moved her hands down to grip his hips, much like he was doing to her. "I like the look of you in jeans."

His smile doubled. "A lot of women get off on me in uniform."

Her smile slipped for a split second but then returned. "Yeah, I try not to enjoy it too much."

"I can tell." He kissed her and pulled her body next to his.

He told himself to go slow. But her kisses were full of demands and passion, and in the end, he couldn't really remember her pulling his clothes off. What he did remember was the feeling of her exposed skin under his fingertips as he removed each article of her clothing.

He admired the way she looked in nothing but a simple cotton bra and panties that rode high up on her hips.

She was a lot sexier than he'd imagined. Her skin was perfect without so much as a freckle on it anywhere. As he ran his hand over her, the contrast of his freckled hand against her smooth skin was like art from two different artists sitting on one canvas.

She was like porcelain and deserved to be treated with care.

He lifted her in his arms and carried her to the bed, where he laid her down gently. He covered her body with his own. After that, his desires for her completely took over his thoughts.

When he slipped a finger under the cotton she was wearing, sexy moans filled his mind.

"Harper, I won't last long if you keep that up," he said after she grabbed his cock and started stroking him slowly.

She stilled, looking up at him. "Do you have condoms?"

He quickly pulled a package from his nightstand and felt her relax. Seeing her naked under him made him want to explore more of her.

Instead of sliding the condom on, he left it on the nightstand and then, using his mouth, traveled down her body until he was nestled between her thighs.

She tasted like spring. Her skin was so soft, he wanted to spend hours enjoying her. However, his own needs had him traveling back up her body as he felt her shiver under him.

He slid on the condom and returned to hover over her. Her long hair was fanned out on his bed, and her dark eyes watched him. Trusted him. Wanted him.

Smiling, he leaned in and kissed her. "Trust me," he whispered as he slid into her.

Always My Love

At that moment, as he lost complete control of himself, he realized that his heart no longer belonged to him. Without realizing it, his feelings for Harper had become so strong that he'd give anything to ensure her safety. Anything.

"I can't move," Harper groaned as she lay half over him a while later. Her hair was lying on his shoulder, and he ran his fingers through the long tresses.

"Then don't," he suggested. "Stay here. I'm sure Lucy and Blue are fast asleep again."

"I should go home." She lifted her head and looked down at him.

The room was darker but the light from the streetlamp outside was enough that they could see one another clearly.

"Should?" he asked, arching his eyebrows. "You don't have work tomorrow, right?"

"Right," she said, resting her fist on his chest and then setting her chin on it.

"I'm off for the next two days. We can do something together tomorrow. Maybe take the dogs to the beach?" he suggested.

She was quiet for a moment. "I should text Hailey and let her know where I am."

"Okay," he said easily as his hand moved down to her lower back. "You can do that, later." He lifted up and kissed her.

Then in a quick move, he spun them around until she was underneath him. Seeing her laugh up at him sent a jolt of energy pulsing through his body.

Waking up with Harper wrapped around him was one of the best feelings he'd ever experienced. It was right up there with the first time Blue had snuggled into his chest at night.

"Morning," Harper said, causing him to wake quickly. He'd expected her to be asleep for a little longer.

"You're awake?" he asked, feeling slightly groggy.

"Yes." She shifted to look down at him. "I heard Lucy bark and was about to slip out of bed to go let them out."

He heard the dogs now and sighed. "We'll go down together."

"Do you have some sweats I can pull on?" she asked as he climbed out of bed.

"Sure." He walked over to his dresser and pulled out a gray army sweatsuit. "Will this do?"

She took it and smiled. "Thanks, I'll be just a minute." She motioned towards the bathroom while he pulled on a matching pair of sweatpants and a T-shirt.

They stood inside the back door and watched the dogs play in the snow and do their business. Neither of them wanted to come back in so they let them play outside while he went and made himself a cup of coffee and then offered her one. He slid open the drawer under the coffee maker to show her all the different flavors he had.

She picked one and then took a cup from the hooks above the counter.

"Creamer?" he asked, opening the fridge. "I have French vanilla and pumpkin spice. Kate left that one over here at Thanksgiving."

"Pumpkin spice sounds good." She took the container from him. "Are your days off always like this?"

"Like what?" he asked, leaning on the counter to sip his coffee.

"So... quiet?" She glanced around the house.

He chuckled. "Now that I have Blue, nothing is quiet. But no. Normally, I'm working on one project or another. I'm helping Kate and Tom fix up their place. They're rebuilding a deck during nice weather and tiling a bathroom. I like to keep busy."

She took a sip of her coffee and smiled. "Oh, I like the pumpkin spice." She held up her mug and then took another sip.

"How about I make us some breakfast?" he suggested.

"I could eat." She smiled and set her mug down, then walked over and wrapped her arms around him. "I think I forgot to thank you for yesterday."

"There was no need." He then brushed his lips across hers. "If you want, you can head up and shower while I cook and let the dogs in."

She smiled. "I'd love that. I've been dying to see how it feels to take a shower in something larger than a coat closet."

"Your shower is that small?"

She nodded. "I'd like your help in rectifying that. When you get around to it." She kissed him.

"I'd be happy to see what I can do."

She kissed him again and then turned and headed up the stairs.

He let the dogs back inside and left them in the laundry room, since they were once again covered in snow. He figured they were just going to get dirty again when they went to the beach in a while. He fed them their breakfast, then got to work on theirs.

Nick liked to cook. It allowed him time to think. Think about Harper and how much she'd changed in the past few weeks.

For as long as she'd been in town, she'd jumped whenever she saw him. But since the day he'd invited her to go with him to get Blue, she'd been different. Maybe it was because she was seeing him as something more than just a cop?

Whatever the reason, he was thankful he'd decided to finally ask her out.

When she came back downstairs, her long hair was wet and she was back in the same clothes she'd worn the day before with the exception that she was still wearing his army sweatshirt.

She looked good in the thing. Looked good in his clothes.

"Wow, something smells wonderful," she said, sitting at the table. "You just made all this?"

"Not the quiche. My mother made a bunch of them, and I keep them in the freezer. She knows they're my favorite." He set down the pan containing the cheese, egg, ham, onion, and jalapeno quiche. "I did chop up the fruit and poured the yogurt. Not to mention I heated the quiche up." He wiggled his eyebrows, trying to impress her. "Still, I do love to cook. Actually, baking is my favorite. My aunt does own a bakery. I spent plenty of summers lending a hand in the kitchen. I can probably make muffins with my eyes shut." He groaned. "Not to mention cookies and pies."

"How did you, Kate, and Brook not grow up weighing a ton? Every time I go into the bakery, I come out with more than I should."

"Well, Kate had her dance. Brook and I had sports. We both played softball, basketball, and soccer." He shrugged. "Plus, for the most part, we grew up eating like this." He motioned to the table.

Suddenly, Harper's smile disappeared as she looked down at her plate.

"I don't remember ever having a homemade meal." Her eyes moved up to his.

His heart sank. "Because your mother was an addict?"

he asked, wanting to know a little more about her childhood.

He knew plenty of addicts. There were a handful he had to deal with in or around Pride. Some didn't care who they hurt. Others he visited at least once a month for domestic calls. But others were good people and good parents. He couldn't make assumptions about Harper's mom.

Harper nodded. "We were lucky if there was any food in the house at all. We hated summers because it meant we couldn't have school meals. That was pretty much the only source of nutrition that we had growing up."

"Surely the state sent someone to check on you. There are plenty of programs—" he started, but he stopped when Harper shook her head.

"We were taught from a young age to hate cops and social workers. We were programmed to run and hide if a strange car drove up to our place. If they asked us at school, we were told to lie. Hailey and I became really good at lying. Then, when we got older, it was just easier not to go to school."

He frowned. "You didn't finish school?"

She frowned down at her hands. "I stopped going when I was sixteen. Hailey was fourteen. I tried to homeschool her, but things were just too hard. We spent most of our time away from the house. To avoid..." She shook her head, then suddenly she jumped up and rushed to the bathroom.

He stood outside and listened to her empty the contents of her stomach.

When she stepped out again, he wrapped his arms around her. "Was it my cooking?" he tried to joke. Thankfully, he heard a soft chuckle from her as she plastered her face against his chest.

"No, I'm sorry. It's just... there's a reason I don't like to talk about my past," she said in a muffled voice.

He nudged her back until she looked up at him. "I'm thankful you opened up to me. It's not necessary, but I will tell you this. It's helpful to have someone you trust to talk to."

She nodded slowly. "I'd like to finish breakfast. If there is more quiche."

He smiled. "Plenty." He took her hand and they walked back to the dining area.

Chapter Nine

She felt like a fool. Every time she thought of what she and Hailey had been through, her stomach turned. Maybe it was the fact that she was, for the first time in her life, opening up to an outsider. Or maybe it was the fact that Nick was a cop? Either way, she'd lost it when she realized she was about to tell him too much.

She figured it was her body's way of stopping her from going too far. Whatever the reason, for the rest of the meal, they chatted about the dogs and what they wanted to do for the rest of the day.

Nick suggested a long walk on the beach to wear the puppies out so they could maybe drive into Edgeview for some shopping and a movie.

She wanted to tell him that she'd never been to a movie theater before, but she didn't want to sound pathetic.

Instead, she eagerly got ready for the walk on the beach.

She'd taken Lucy on a few walks but not on the beach since they were miles away, further up in the hills that surrounded Pride.

Their hikes had been through trees and the fields that surrounded the cabin.

Her dog took to the beach like she was born for it. When Harper said so, Nick pointed out that the Stevens most likely used to take the puppies to the beach, since they lived as close to the water as he did.

While they walked almost a full mile down the beach, Nick talked about the town. He filled her in on each house that they passed, as if he knew she needed to keep her mind off what had happened earlier. She was thankful for that.

When she'd taken Lucy on walks in the past, it had only taken a few moments to clean the dirt off her paws. But when they returned to Nick's house, both dogs were completely covered in wet sand, and packed snow stuck to their fur.

Nick hosed each dog down, and she dried them off with towels that he provided. When the two of them were dry, they climbed into the kennel and fell fast asleep.

"I think they like being together," she pointed out.

"Yeah, it's nice for now. I've scheduled a vet appointment for Blue to have his baby-making parts removed." He sighed. "It's best that he does not reproduce, especially since it appears he'll be spending a lot of time with his sister and other siblings. Reece got one of Blue's brothers and is getting him fixed. He named him Muhammad Ali. Ali for short." He smiled. "Anyway, he mentioned it the other day so I set an appointment for Blue as well. He goes in to get neutered when he's old enough."

"Poor boy," Harper said, looking down at the dog. "I suppose I should look into getting Lucy fixed too. I am not ready to be a grandmom," she said with a chuckle.

"How about I go up and change and then we can head to Edgeview?" he suggested.

"I'd like that." She tried not to sound too eager.

While he went upstairs to change out of the sweats, she took a moment to freshen up in the downstairs bathroom. Thankfully, she always carried a little makeup and a hairbrush with her in her bag.

After applying the basics of makeup, she decided her hair was too tangled from the wind on the beach, so she pulled it to one side and braided it in a loose braid. Then she pulled on the beanie she kept in her bag. She looked presentable.

Nick came back downstairs in a pair of worn jeans and a sweater. He was carrying both of their shoes from the day before.

"Thanks." She took her shoes from him and sat down to put them on.

"What movie would you like to see?" he asked as he tied his shoes.

She shrugged and asked, "What's playing?"

He pulled out his phone when he was done tying his shoes and then rattled off a few titles. She hadn't heard of any of them so suggested he pick the movie. She was okay with whatever.

She was trying desperately to hide the fact that she was just thrilled to be going to an actual theater.

"The new *Mission Impossible* sounds good," he suggested.

"Sounds good to me."

"It's still snowing. We'll take the Jeep if that's okay?" he said as they pulled on their coats.

"Sure," she said, following him through the light snow.

Once again, he opened her car door for her. She'd never had anyone do that before but had seen the move in a few movies she'd watched at home.

In her youth, she'd never once dreamed of a boy making romantic gestures for her. Since the moment she'd turned thirteen, the only thing she had thought about boys or men was to fear them.

She held in a shiver but apparently not too well because Nick reached over and turned the heater up a couple notches.

"Better?" he asked.

"Yes, thanks." She tried to keep her mind free of her past.

"Why did you become a cop after you got out of the military?" she asked. He'd told her all about the boy he used to be. Now she wanted to know more about the man he was.

He glanced sideways at her as he turned on the main highway that led towards the next biggest town.

"Well, two years after I joined the army, I became an MP. Military police," he clarified.

"The military have their own police?" she asked, feeling stupid.

He nodded and continued to talk as if her question wasn't stupid. He told her all about how he'd become an MP. What his job entailed while he was in the military.

Everything except the darkness that haunted him. The thing that had caused him to leave the military and return to Pride.

Since she was keeping her own secrets, she figured he was due his.

When they parked at the mall in Edgeview, she felt a rush of nerves race through her as they headed inside.

She'd been to the mall once or twice in the time she'd lived in Pride. Normally she'd just run inside to get an item or two. She didn't like to be around so many people.

"We can head inside and get our movie tickets and

snacks or shop first. There's a showing at noon and another one at one."

"Let's go to the earlier show," she suggested. "Then we can do some shopping after."

"Sounds perfect." He took her hand and they started walking towards the theater together.

Everything was so new to her. She watched Nick purchase the tickets and felt a rush as they handed them over. They headed towards the snack counter.

Theater popcorn smelled and tasted so much better than any of those bags she'd made in the microwave. Even the soda they shared tasted better.

They took their snacks and headed down a long hallway lined with large cutouts and posters for other movies. Nick held the door open for her and followed her into the darkness.

"Where do you normally sit?" he asked as they stood at the base of the rows of chairs.

"I... haven't been to a movie before," she admitted, too in awe at the entire experience to remember to lie.

"What?" Nick frowned. "Ever?"

She glanced over at him and shook her head. "Nope." She figured she'd already told him too much so why lie about this. "First timer here." She smiled.

"Damn, maybe I should have taken you to a better movie?"

"This is perfect. Where is the best place to sit? At the top?"

"No, actually, you want the center of the screen to be at eye level. We'll sit just up there."

She followed him up a few rows and then to the middle of the seating row.

"This is perfect." She set her drink in the hole of the

armrest. "The chairs even rock." She smiled as she rocked back and forth.

He chuckled. "One of these theaters serves you dinner while you watch the movie. We should have gone to that one."

"This is perfect." She touched his arm. "How do they get this popcorn to taste so good?"

He chuckled. "Butter and a ton of salt." He grabbed a handful and ate some while she did the same.

For the next few hours, she sat in complete awe at the experience. Every moment of it.

Nick held her hand through most of it when they weren't enjoying their snacks.

By the time the credits were rolling, she was determined to bring her sister to a movie soon.

"That was really amazing," she said as they walked out of the theater.

"I'm glad you enjoyed it." He brushed his lips across hers. "How about we grab some lunch at the food court?"

"Okay." She took his hand as they strolled out of the theater.

"Normally this place is crowded on days like this, but thankfully, winter break is over and school started up again today," he said as they walked through the mall. "I came here just before Christmas with my sister and this place was packed."

"Hailey and I came down here on Black Friday." She rolled her eyes. "It was crazy too."

"I don't normally shop on Black Friday. Now Cyber Monday, that's my jam."

She chuckled. "I don't even have a computer at home."

"You don't?" He frowned when she shook her head.

"My phone is all I need for now," she said as they stepped into the food court.

"What'll it be?" he asked, glancing around the court at all their options.

"I like the noodle place." She motioned. "And the chicken place. Then again there's always pizza."

In the end, they settled on the noodle place she liked and sat in the almost empty food court and enjoyed their meal.

After eating, they walked around the mall, dipping into shops either of them wanted to. She purchased a cute sweater for Lucy, and Nick got Blue a bright blue collar and leash combo.

Almost an hour after the movie had ended, they headed home. The snow had gotten a lot deeper, but the streets looked clear enough.

"I guess it's a good thing we didn't stay in there much longer," Nick pointed out.

"I'm not a big shopper."

"Growing up, this was the place to be. I'm sure you spent loads of wasted time strolling through a mall."

"Nope, up until we moved here, I'd never been in a mall before," she admitted. Nick remained quiet as he opened the Jeep door for her. "I never had a man open a car door for me either, until you."

He held her still and pulled her into his arms. Her knees almost went weak at his gentle touch.

"I like to hear all about your firsts." He brushed his lips across hers. "I'd like to hear the things you've never experienced and give them to you." He kissed her again, and this time her knees did go weak.

Just then a horn blasted as someone shouted at them to get a room.

Chuckling, Nick released his hold on her and she climbed into the Jeep.

They had just turned off the main road in town and were heading towards the small highway that would take them to Pride when a school bus directly in front of them slid off the road. She screamed as she watched the massive thing hit the ditch and roll several times.

Harper had a moment to brace as the Jeep slid to a halt, stopping only a few yards from the bus that had finally landed on its side.

"Call 911," Nick said, then he jumped out of the car and raced towards the bus.

With shaky hands, she pulled out her phone and called while watching Nick pull open the twisted doors to the bus.

After giving the dispatcher their location and the emergency information, she jumped out of the Jeep.

Hearing children scream and cry, she raced to help.

Nick had gotten the back doors open and she climbed in. There were several children, no older than twelve, crawling over the seats towards her as Nick encouraged them to keep going.

"Here," she called out. "Come to me." She helped a little boy climb over the last seat. Then she set him down in the snow as someone called out to her.

"Here." A woman rushed towards her. "I've got blankets."

"Take him. There's more," she told the woman, then she turned to help another boy.

She lost count of the kids she helped out. Most of them were covered in cuts, bruises, and blood. Lots of blood.

One boy around nine was holding a very broken arm to his chest. She carefully handed him to a man who had stopped to help as well.

One girl around eight, who was wearing a bright red jumpsuit, couldn't walk on her leg so Nick carried her through the overturned bus seats and handed her over.

"The bus driver is dead," he told her in a soft voice. "I think she's the last of the kids. I'm going to go make sure I've got everyone."

Harper nodded and turned to carry the child to where the rest of the children were huddled together.

Just then, the ambulance and firetruck pulled to a stop beside Nick's Jeep and more chaos ensued.

She placed the little girl in the arms of a fireman, who rushed her towards an ambulance.

She was asked her name and whether she'd been on the bus, as well as who else was in the bus.

Just then, Nick climbed out of the back of the bus empty-handed and rushed over to answer as many questions as he could. Thankfully, he seemed to know a few of the responders and the questions aimed at her stopped.

A thermal blanket was wrapped around her when one of the firemen noticed her shaking.

Up until that point, she hadn't realized she'd been cold. Then her teeth started chattering and her fingers, nose, and ears grew so cold that she doubted she could feel anything.

"We're done," Nick told her as he wrapped his arms around her. "Come on, let's get you warmed up back in the Jeep. They have our contact information if they have more questions."

He helped her back to the Jeep and opened the door for her.

When the heater finally kicked on, she melted into the seat and fell fast asleep as he drove them back to Pride.

Chapter Ten

Nick drove the Jeep cautiously all the way back home. He knew without a doubt that the bus had slipped on black ice. He'd hit the same patch and, thankfully, had gotten the Jeep back under control before they'd ended up in the ditch as well.

Twenty-three kids. There had been twenty-three kids under the age of twelve on that bus who had almost lost their lives. Instead, only one older gentleman, the bus driver, had died today.

Nick had gotten used to jumping into action during chaotic times while in the military. Jumping into the bus had been second nature to him. He hadn't been squeamish when he'd seen what the accident had done to the driver. Still, he hadn't wanted any of the kids or Harper to witness the horror.

Harper had fallen asleep. No doubt she'd gone into shock after the entire ordeal was over. Still, he'd been impressed that she'd kept it together long enough to help him get all the kids out and safe.

"Do you think they're okay?" Harper asked after he pulled into his driveway and shut off the Jeep.

"Yeah, a couple of broken bones, some cuts and bruises. But twenty-three kids will get to sleep in their own beds tonight, safe and sound."

"Thanks to you," Harper said, taking his hand in hers.

"And you," he pointed out. "I know you work tomorrow, but I was hoping..." He pulled her close.

"I'll stay. I already sent Hailey a text." She smiled. "I don't go into work until eleven. I should have plenty of time to head home and get ready."

He kissed her. "How about we go inside, grab a shower, then I'll make us some popcorn and we can watch a movie with the dogs?"

"Sounds wonderful." She sighed.

"I can throw your clothes in the wash."

She nodded, and then to his horror, she burst out crying. He pulled her as close as he could.

"I'm being stupid," she said against his chest.

"No," he kept saying as he stroked her hair.

"Those kids. They were all so scared. I used to be scared too. I remember being so afraid to go home. So afraid of Heidi. So afraid of Fred."

He wanted to ask her who Heidi and Fred were, but he just let her mumble on about her childhood fears. Most of it he couldn't understand, but he clearly heard some words and tried to hold in his anger as she mentioned how her mother would abuse her and Hailey. Then she mentioned something that had his arms tightening around her and broke the spell.

"I'm sorry," she said, jerking in his arms. He let her pull away and watched her as she wiped her hands over her face. "I didn't mean to..." She shook her head.

"Share?" He nodded. "I get it." He took her hand in his. "Let's head inside." He knew she was probably thinking of a million excuses to leave now.

He didn't want her to go. Not because she'd dropped her guard for a moment and let loose some of the darkness that held her back. He wanted to know more, but the look in her eyes told him that she wasn't ready.

She nodded after a moment, and he jumped out of the Jeep before she could change her mind.

When they walked into the house, the dogs were so happy to see them. Harper hugged Lucy as the dog licked the dry tears off her face.

He let them out as they stripped the soiled clothes off themselves. He told Harper to head up to the shower while he waited for the dogs to return. She nodded and, after wrapping a robe he had hanging in the laundry room around herself, she headed up the stairs.

When the dogs returned, he went upstairs, not caring that he was only in his boxers. Instead of leaving the dogs locked in the laundry room, he let them roam the house. Their feet were wet, but otherwise they were fairly clean. He knew that Harper would need their company.

He stepped into the shower and pulled her into his arms, holding onto her while the hot water washed over them.

"I'm so sorry you had to go through all that," he said into her wet hair. "I'm sorry today brought up bad memories for you."

She shook her head. "It didn't. Not really. It just stings knowing those kids will have bad memories from today."

"You helped calm them down. They're going to remember the kind woman who helped when they needed it."

She smiled up at him. "Thank you. That helps." Then she leaned up on her toes and kissed him.

"I know it's probably bad timing, but I've never had sex in a shower before." She ran her hands over him.

He smiled and nudged her back against the tile wall. "I'd be very happy to show you the ropes." He wiggled his eyebrows and had her laughing.

Then he kissed her and the sounds of her laughter turned into soft moans. He ran his hands over her wet skin.

Her fingers tightened in his wet hair as he took the kiss deeper, letting all of the feelings he had for her build up and pour out when he touched her.

She was everything he wanted. Everything he'd hoped for.

This. This was what happiness was. He wanted to show her everything that he felt.

He lifted her up slightly and held her against the tile wall. He hoisted her leg up over his hip so he could give her more pleasure. When he dipped his fingers into her, just watching her explode with pleasure was reward enough.

Then she reached for him and all he could think about was being inside her. He was about to do just that when he remembered he hadn't brought a condom into the shower.

Shutting off the water, he lifted Harper into his arms and carried her out of the shower. When he almost slipped on the wet tile, he decided they'd gone far enough. He set her down on the countertop and grabbed a condom from his bathroom drawer before stepping between her legs.

When he finally slipped inside her, he couldn't hold back any longer and let his demands fully take over. His fingers dug into her skin. His kisses were deeper than before.

He knew he wasn't as gentle as he should be, but this

was primal. This was the need to feel alive. The need to take what he needed as much as give her what she wanted.

The moment he felt her convulse around him, he shouted with his own release and felt his entire body go numb.

"Are you okay?" Harper asked softly next to his ear.

"Hm," he groaned, still holding himself inside her.

Harper chuckled softly. "I know we ate a while ago, but I'm hungry again."

He leaned back and smiled at her as his own stomach responded at the thought of food.

"Yeah, me too." He smiled "Are you okay now?"

She nodded then leaned up and kissed him. "Much better now."

"I'll get you those sweats." He wrapped a towel around his waist as he headed towards his bedroom.

Half an hour later, Harper sat at his bar top and watched him cook grilled cheese and turkey sandwiches. He was heating up a can of potato soup while she sipped a mug of hot chocolate.

"I have some frozen cookie dough my aunt stocks in my freezer. I could throw some in the oven for later?" he suggested while he flipped the sandwich.

"Sounds great. I'll get it." She walked into the laundry room and came back with a tub of pre-made, pre-cut, frozen cookie dough. "This is amazing. Everything in your freezer is labeled."

He smiled. "I got a labeler for Christmas. And I was bored one night."

"Your aunt made all of this?" she asked when she opened the tub of small round cookie dough pieces.

"Yeah, she keeps me stocked with all the sweets." He chuckled. "Kate calls Becca her sugar dealer."

Harper laughed as she turned on his oven. "Cookie sheets?"

He motioned to the thin cupboard next to his oven. "Pan spray is there." He pointed at another cupboard.

It was nice, moving around the kitchen with Harper. After she slid the loaded cookie sheet into the oven, he handed her a plate and a bowl and they headed to the table to eat.

Blue sat next to him and begged while Lucy lay down on the dog bed in the living room.

"Okay, I can see the merit of not giving him human food while we're eating." He snapped his fingers and pointed to the dog bed.

Blue sat on his butt and tilted his head at him as if to say that he didn't understand what he wanted.

"Bed," Nick said in a firm tone.

The dog let out a sigh and a little bark, as if he was talking back.

"Now," Nick told him.

Blue turned and went and lay down next to Lucy with a loud groan.

"I won that round." He smiled.

At the sound of his happy tone, Blue jumped up and sat once more at his feet.

Nick sighed and repeated the whole ordeal. This time, after his dog was settled with Lucy, Nick smiled and continued eating his dinner. Harper gave him some good advice while they ate, little things that he could do to train Blue.

Once they were done eating, he pulled the cookies from the oven and took a plate of them into the living room.

"Want to watch a movie up here or down in the basement?" he asked.

"Here is fine. Maybe we can get a fire going?"

He chuckled and walked over to flip on the gas fireplace with a remote.

"Nice. I should install one of these at my place." She sat down on the sofa.

He sat down next to her and held the cookie plate up for her to take one. He flipped on the television and was shocked when an image from earlier of Harper holding a little girl in a red jumpsuit filled the screen.

"What's this?" Harper sat forward with a frown.

Suddenly, her phone rang. He hit pause on the news report, knowing he could hit play again and watch the full report after she was done talking. Seeing Harper and the little girl covered in blood on the big screen somehow made it all feel so... strange. As if he was seeing the scene through someone else's eyes.

Harper looked so determined in the image. So loving towards the little girl she didn't even know. Just the way the little girl was looking up at Harper had his heart swealing with love.

"It's Hailey," Harper said before answering the call. "Hi." She paused and then said. "Yes, we're fine." She glanced at him.

She shifted and he listened while Harper filled Hailey in on what had happened earlier.

When she got off the phone, he hit continue and they watched the full news report about the bus accident.

"The driver, David Gillard, sixty-eight years old, life-long resident of Edgeview and a retired social studies teacher, died at the scene.

"Twenty-three grade school children were all recovering thanks to the heroics of two people, an off-duty Pride police officer, Nick Farrow, and Harper Davis, a bartender at the Golden Oar in Pride."

He was happy that the report was quick and accurate. When it was over, he paused the television again and looked over to see Harper pale.

"Hey, are you okay?" he asked, pulling her close.

"I... is this local or national?" she asked.

He glanced at the screen. "Local. Why?"

She seemed to relax at that bit of news.

"I..." She took a deep breath, then turned towards him. "I don't want my past catching up with me," she said clearly.

"Okay." He took her hands in his. "What does that mean?"

"Just that... if a particular person saw that report, they would know not only what town I live in, but where I work," she said slowly, as if trying to weigh each of her words carefully.

"Okay," he said, slowly understanding. "Are you in any danger?"

She waited for what seemed a very long time before answering. "No, it's just a local report." She took a deep breath.

He nodded. "If you were, would you tell me?" he asked, trying not to feel slightly hurt.

Her eyes met his. "Yes," she said clearly. "I think my days of jumping when I see you are over." She laid her hand on his face gently. "I trust you. I trust that you trust me." She smiled and, even though he saw the hesitation she still had, he decided to let it slide for now.

Chapter Eleven

When she walked into work the next day, the last thing Harper expected was getting cheered for. Everyone in the restaurant—employees and customers alike—stood up and clapped when they noticed her.

She felt her face heat as she quickly ducked behind the bar. Then she saw the flowers with her name on them and melted.

Reading the card, she smiled and then laughed.

"Thinking of you today. You're my hero. –Nick"

She knew he had the day off. When she'd left him and Blue that morning to go home to shower and change into her work clothes, the pair had been heading to the beach for a long walk.

"So, who are those from?" Connie asked. Connie was another bartender. The woman had hired Harper and was easily the nicest person to work under Harper had ever had.

"None of your business," Harper joked, tucking the flowers under the bar.

"Honey, it's a small town." Connie smiled. "Everyone knows they're from Nick."

"Yeah, I figured." Harper laughed. "Still, it was worth a shot. You know, keeping my love life a secret."

"Not in Pride. Nothing stays a secret for long. Hey, did you hear your little heroics made national news?"

Harper's heart felt like it stopped beating for a full ten seconds. "What?"

"That report was aired on the big networks first thing this morning. They're calling the pair of you true heroes," Connie said, then she went to fill someone's order.

Harper wanted to run. To hide. To shout. To punch something. Instead, she put her fears aside and got to work since the lunch rush was just starting.

During her first break, she called her sister.

"That report when national," she said when Hailey answered her phone.

"It did?" Hailey sounded excited at first, then asked. "Do you think he saw it?"

"I don't want to take any chances. From now on, we stick close. I won't spend any more nights at Nick's away from you," Harper said, feeling a little sad. She'd really enjoyed the past two nights lying in Nick's arms. Waking up to him beside her.

"Don't put your life on hold because you're afraid for me," Hailey said firmly. "I can take care of myself now."

"No, you can't," Harper hissed.

"Yes, I can. I'm... I'm signing up to take self-defense and boxing lessons from Reece."

Harper's eyes narrowed slightly. "Reece Crawford?"

"Yes," Hailey answered happily. "I just talked to him earlier today. He's agreed to teach me how to box."

Harper felt a little better knowing her sister might be

able to protect herself. Still, she knew that what was coming for them wouldn't hesitate, while Hailey would. She always had. Her sister froze when things turned... crazy. It was the number one reason Harper had always looked out for her little sister.

One of the reasons she hadn't paused when jumping in to help the kids escape the school bus. Her first instincts were to help. To protect those who couldn't. To fight whatever evil was hunting its prey.

And Harper and Hailey had been the prey.

"I don't like it," Harper finally said. "Still, I think it's a good thing you learn some self-defense," she admitted. "But neither of us are left alone from here on. We should ride to work together..."

Hailey's groan stopped her. "This is Pride. I can't sneeze without someone we know saying bless you." Hailey was quiet for a moment. "What have you told Nick?"

"Not..." Someone came out of the back door of the restaurant and lit a cigarette. "Not everything. I have to get back to work," she said quickly. "I'll be home tonight."

"Okay." She waited. "Harper, he's not coming for us."

Harper wished clear down to her bones that it was true. She'd give anything for the man who had tortured them to leave them alone for the rest of their lives. But this was Fred, and Fred was a monster.

If there was one thing that she had learned from all the horror movies she'd seen, monsters usually came back for the prey when they least expect it.

Now was that time. She and Hailey were officially settled in Pride. They were happy.

She was dating a man, something she'd never allowed herself to do. Ever.

Hailey and she were happy with their jobs. Happy with their home. They had plans. A future. Possibilities.

None of these things had ever even registered in their lives before now. Why wouldn't Fred come and take everything away from them. It's what he did. Though there was no way Fred could know about their uncle's place, right? He had never taken a real interest in their mother's family.

Nine years ago, he'd swooped into their little hell and turned everything upside down. He'd taken things from bad to worse.

Instead of being ignored by an addictive mother and occasionally slapped around when they mouthed off, they'd graduated to cowering in fear every moment of their lives.

The girls had to endure things that most children didn't even know existed. Things that would break most adults.

The only thing that had gotten them through it was each other. And now, the only thing that would get them through what was coming—and Harper knew without a doubt that it was coming—was each other.

No matter how wonderful Nick had been in the past few days, he was a cop. Facts were still facts.

Harper was a murderer. Someday, when Fred found them, the truth would come out, and Nick would have to do what he'd sworn he'd do when he became a police officer. Uphold the law.

She supposed it was for the best. It was only a matter of time before she confided in him. After all, she'd had several moments of weakness and had told him far too much already.

It would be better to break things off with him before they could get too serious and leave her brokenhearted.

Who was she fooling? She was already brokenhearted.

By the end of her shift, she'd talked herself into breaking

things off with Nick permanently. She'd tried to convince herself that she didn't love him. But in truth, she had loved him the moment she'd seen him out of his uniform and snuggling with a puppy.

But she didn't trust herself around him. Didn't trust that she wouldn't tell him everything. Every horrible detail. Every moment of her and Hailey's terrible childhood.

Then, she'd tell him about that night. That last night she and Hailey had spent in the hut they had called home all of their young lives.

The thought of him turning away from her hurt her more than the thought of her walking away from him. She didn't think she could bear it if he looked at her differently than he did now.

If he knew what she was, it would break her.

Since she knew Hailey was working the late shift at Baked and wouldn't be home for another hour, she stopped by Nick's place on her way home from work.

In her mind, she planned a quick exit.

She was going to knock on his door and say her peace on his doorstep. Tell him things were off between them. Simple.

She'd never broken up with anyone before. It couldn't be too hard. Right?

Just tell him thanks for the few nights of fun but it was over.

Simple.

Only the moment Nick opened his door in work-out shorts and a T-shirt, covered in sweat, she forgot what she had planned to say and blurted out, "I can't see you anymore."

She held her breath, trying to hide all of her emotions.

Nick's eyebrows rose slightly. "Okay, why don't you

come in and tell me what this is about?" He held the door open for her.

She told herself not to cross the threshold. That if she did, there would be no going back.

Instead of saying no, she walked right inside like a sheep to the slaughter.

When he shut the door behind him, she hugged herself and lifted her chin.

"I think it's best if we don't continue seeing one another," she said, trying to sound firm.

"Why?" Nick asked, using a towel to wipe the sweat from his forehead.

God, he looked so sexy all sweaty. Why? Why did he look so sexy this way?

"Because. Listen, I know we had fun, but..."

"Fun?" Nick took a step towards her, his tone a low warning.

"Sure," she continued on, not seeing the threat right in front of her. "I mean, it was fun. We're just too different. I can't afford to be distracted from my goals. It's best to call it quits before things between us get complicated. Besides, my sister needs me and I'm all she has."

There. She'd said her peace. This was simple. Now all she had to do was leave before the tears started.

"No," Nick responded, throwing her off balance.

"No?" she asked, slowly.

"No. You're not going to get off this easy." He motioned towards the sofa. "Sit. Tell me what this is all about."

"No," she threw back at him. "You don't get that. What you get is what I gave you. I want this to end." She nodded once.

"No," he said softly.

She growled and threw her hands up. "Why not?"

She thought she saw his lips twitch. "Because you owe me a better explanation. Because whether or not you want to believe it, things between us are already complicated."

He took two quick steps towards her and took her shoulders in his hands. He pulled her to his chest and covered her mouth with his.

The kiss started out rough, demanding. From the first moment of contact, her entire body melted.

He was right. Things were already complicated between them.

Somewhere in the past few days, she'd lost control of herself and had given everything she had to him.

"Nick?" she sighed when he softened the kiss.

"I can't afford for you to leave now," Nick said softly into her ear. "You'd take part of me with you."

She closed her eyes as tears slid down her cheeks. "I need to protect Hailey," she said, almost begging for him to understand.

She felt him tense slightly. "Does this have something to do with the news report going national?"

Swallowing, she nodded.

She felt Nick take a deep breath.

"Are you safe?" he asked.

"We are, just as long as I don't spend any more nights away from home."

Nick was quiet for a moment.

"Go home, Harper. But this isn't over," he warned as he took a step back. "When you're ready to open up to me, completely, let me know and I'll be here. "

She felt her knees go weak, and for a moment she wanted to blurt out everything to him if it meant that he would kiss her again the way he had moments before.

Then, reality caused her feet to move quickly out the door.

She was halfway home when the numbness wore off. She made it into the house before her knees gave out and she cried tears like she had never experienced before.

Hailey found her there when she got home. Without asking, her sister pulled her into her arms and held onto her for as long as they both needed one another.

Chapter Twelve

At first, Nick avoided going into the Golden Oar. He was hurt and angry that Harper had tried to break things off with him. Hurt and angry that she wouldn't open up to him about her reasoning. Even though he'd told her and himself that he didn't need to know her past, it still stung.

Then he remembered that he had a dark past that she knew nothing about as well.

How could he expect her to open up to him when he hadn't opened up to her.

It was obvious now that she was protecting her sister. Without her knowing, he'd driven by their cabin and Hailey's work a few more times whenever he was on shift.

Tom noticed on the second day and asked him why. He shrugged it off and told him he was just making sure there weren't any crazies that had seen the news report and would go after Harper or her sister.

By the second week of not seeing Harper, he was dying inside. He was grumpy all the time. He no longer took Blue on long walks and instead just sat in the yard while the dog whined and sniffed, as if looking for Lucy and Harper.

Damn. Even his dog was missing them.

Two days later, when his shift was over, Tom slugged him on the shoulder and nudged him towards his Jeep.

"Go. You have the day off tomorrow, and I know for a fact that Harper has the night off and tomorrow as well. Go up to the cabin. Set things straight. Whatever happened between the pair of you can't be as bad as having to deal with your foul mood."

He opened his mouth to argue, but then Tom glared at him. "Or I could have your sister call you and tell you the same thing?"

Nick groaned. "Fine, I'll... go up there to check on her," he added as he started towards his Jeep.

He kept trying to convince himself that he was only going to swing by and check up on Lucy. He stopped off at his place and picked up Blue and changed out of his uniform.

After all, he didn't want the first time she saw him in weeks for her to jump because he was in his uniform.

When they pulled into her driveway, he was thankful to see Hailey's old truck missing.

When the sisters had first arrived in town, they'd only had the one car. After a few months, Hailey had purchased the old truck from one of the Jordans. It took a while for everyone in town to realize the old thing had a new owner.

When he knocked on the door, Blue let out a happy bark. Instantly, he could hear Lucy's return greeting and smiled.

Harper would have to open the door now. He knew she wouldn't want to keep the brother and sister apart.

"You don't play fair," Harper said the moment she opened her door.

The dogs happily jumped and pawed at one another.

"I hadn't planned on this. I just knew that Blue missed her," he said with a smile. "Honest."

Harper was wearing a white T-shirt with what appeared to be splattered paint on it. Her long hair was up in a messy bun, and her worn jeans had holes in the knees.

God, she looked good.

"Are we interrupting you?" he asked.

She groaned and held the door open after Blue followed Lucy inside. She motioned for him to come in when he just stood there.

"You might as well come in," she added.

He smiled and stepped inside.

He'd never been inside the cabin before and was surprised at how nice it was. At least what he could see so far. Sure, it was dated. Wood paneling on the walls. Built-in bookcases and cupboards. An old woodstove.

But the hardwood flooring was shiny and appeared to have a fresh coat of stain on it. The walls in the attached kitchen looked like they had been painted recently as well. The furniture was used but in nice condition.

The dogs happily chased one another through the living room and dining area.

"Well, since you're here, would you like some iced tea? I was just pouring some for myself." Before he could answer, she turned and walked through the dining room.

Curious, he followed her through the room and into the kitchen.

The old cupboards had a new coat of white paint on them, making the countertops and the rest of the kitchen appear newer. If it wasn't for the old appliances, he would have never known the kitchen was so dated.

"I guess it's really true. Everything old is new again." He motioned to the farmhouse sink.

She glanced over her shoulder and then smiled. "We lucked out that my uncle hadn't changed much in the cabin since it was built. Do you know how much sinks like this run now?"

He nodded. "Yeah, I priced one out for my kitchen. Too much." He shook his head. "Are you painting?" He motioned to her clothes.

She glanced down at herself and sighed. "No, I'm learning to tile." She rolled her eyes. "I got it in my head to remodel our bathroom."

"Yourself?" He frowned. "You should have called..." He dropped off when she glared at him. "Right, well." He rolled up his sleeves. "I'm here now. Let me take a look at—"

"I can do it myself," Harper said, firmly.

"I don't doubt that," he agreed. "But why not take some expert help when you can get it?"

She leaned on the counter and took a sip of the iced tea she'd just poured herself. "Fine," she said when she was done. "Back here." She set her glass down and started walking down a short hallway.

He followed her, trying not to look in each bedroom he passed. Which one was hers? The one with the soft teal walls or the darker sky-blue walls?

He could imagine her style being the softer color.

The bathroom sat at the end of the hallway and was a complete mess. It appeared that she had knocked out a half wall to expand the shower. Thankfully, he didn't see any electric or plumbing in the wall. There were chunks of tile sticking to the new shower walls but most were slipping down or lying on the floor of what would be her new shower.

"I've been watching videos." She motioned towards her phone, which was sitting on the sink area.

"Do you want my help?" he asked, turning towards her.

She frowned and then blew a piece of her hair out of her eyes. "At this point, I'm desperate for a shower." She threw up her hands.

He smiled and walked over to pull off the rest of the tiles she'd put on the wall.

"First off, we need to clean all this up," he said.

"But—" she started, but when he glanced back at her in question, she rolled her eyes. "I'll get a trash can."

They spent the next hour emptying the mess in the bathroom. Then, after he suggested removing the small sink area and rearranging the bathroom, they tore out the vanity until there was nothing left except the toilet.

Once the entire room was empty, he walked around and checked the existing plumbing and electric for options. Then he drew out his ideas on a piece of paper and estimated what the final cost would be.

They had removed the small single-sink vanity, simple square box shower, and a large, oversized cabinet space, which she'd already destroyed before he'd gotten there. There was room now for a double sink vanity, so each sister could have a sink with drawers on each side. Along with a much larger walk-in shower with tile walls, there would still be room enough for a small linen closet behind the bathroom door.

Harper jumped at the idea of having the massive shower that he showed her and told him that she and Hailey would figure out the cost of it all.

"How long do you think it will take to complete the

work?" Harper asked once they had agreed on a plan for the room.

He thought about it. "Not long. Less than a week. Maybe less if I can get the days off from work. Tom owes me a few favors and might fill in for my on-call shifts."

She bit her bottom lip and then he watched her shoulders lift slightly. "Okay, I'll call and see if I can take the time off. Let's do this," she said cheerfully. "What do we need to start?"

"First, I have to go borrow my dad's truck and some power tools. Then we hit the hardware store." He pulled out his phone and shot a text to his father, who immediately replied.

"You know where the keys are. Fill it up with gas when you return it."

Nick smiled and slipped his phone back in his pocket.

"How about a trip to the hardware store?" he asked Harper.

Thankfully, Pride's Hardware and Lumber Yard, had everything they needed, including a rustic double vanity and sinks that Harper liked. She picked out more of the tile that she wanted in the shower, a simple off-white tile with tan undertones, along with tan grout.

She even purchased two new wood-framed mirrors for over the dual sinks.

He, on the other hand, spent more of his time in the lumber section. He grabbed two-by-fours to build up the walls to separate the toilet and shower area from the sink area so that the sisters didn't have to fight over the bathroom as much. According to Harper, it was the biggest issues they had living in the cabin, since it only had one bathroom.

He also grabbed the Hardie board that would line the walls of the showers under the tiles. He made sure to get everything he'd need to build the walls—nails, caulk, mud, and grout—and helped Harper pick out the color of paint that would go on the walls after all the work was done.

Since it would be cheaper to tile the floor after they were done, instead of repairing the old wood floors, she picked out rectangle wood-look tile that matched the coloring of the tile in the shower.

When they returned to her place with the truck loaded, Hailey was already home.

"What have you done to our bathroom?" Hailey said when they walked inside. When she saw Nick, she smiled. "Hi, Nick."

"Hi." He smiled and turned to Harper. "I'm going to start bringing everything inside."

Harper nodded in his direction, and he heard her start to explain to her sister why their one and only bathroom was out of commission for possibly the next week.

When he came back in, carrying an armful of tiles, Hailey stood in the kitchen drinking a soda.

"I'm sorry she dragged you into this," Hailey said.

"She didn't drag. I jumped at the opportunity to help out. I think seeing what I accomplished at my place sparked her interest and her jealousy." He smiled.

"Oh, I'd heard you'd fixed up your place. Actually, there are a handful of old homes in town that have undergone remodeling in Pride. I guess having a new home subdivision close to town has forced a lot of people to upgrade their older homes," Hailey said with a shrug.

"That and a lot of my friends and family are getting married. Younger couples are flooding into town and taking something old and making it home. Like the two of you," he added, thinking of a few new people that had either married in the past few years or had moved into Pride.

"Look at this place. How long did it sit empty until you came along?"

Hailey glanced around the room they were standing in. "My great-uncle moved here in his twenties and then lived the rest of his life here. He died around five years ago."

He frowned slightly, not wanting her to see it, and turned away to set the boxes he'd carried inside down. He was getting more information from Hailey than he had so far from her sister about their move to Pride.

Everyone had assumed that Hank Davis had been their uncle. He supposed it didn't matter if he was actually their great-uncle.

"What made you decide to move in?" he asked, trying to sound casual.

Hailey shrugged her shoulders and then walked over to toss the empty soda can in the trash. "It was empty and we needed a place. But finding our jobs was the key to staying." She smiled. "I like working at Baked and, as far as I can tell, Harper likes the Golden Oar."

"It's a job," Harper said from the doorway. "Are you going to stick around and help us?" she asked her sister.

"Nope, I was just swinging by to shower and change. Now, I suppose, I'll have to settle for showering down at the Boys and Girls club. I've got my first self-defense and boxing lessons from Reece," Hailey answered.

"Good." Harper glanced at him.

"Reece is going to teach self-defense at the club?" For the past few years, several people had tried to talk him into it but none so far had succeeded in persuading him to.

"I'm his first guinea pig," Hailey said, then she disappeared down the hallway into the darker blue room.

"Should I be worried?" Harper asked quietly.

"About Reece?" Nick's eyebrows rose in question.

Harper shrugged. "I don't know him very well. He's not a drinker and doesn't hang out at the bar."

"Reece is one of the best guys in town your sister could spend time with," he reassured her. "Wyatt, Reece, and I, along with a bunch of the Jordans, were like the A-Team in Pride. If we saw injustice, we were usually the ones to fix it."

He picked up the box of tile and carried it towards the bathroom.

"What do we do first?" she asked after they finished unloading everything.

"Now we build the new shower walls and the wall to separate the toilet and sinks from the rest of the room." He motioned to the lumber.

"What can I do?" she asked, biting her bottom lip.

He thought about it. "I can show you how to use the table saw." He motioned to the saw he'd set up in the hallway. It was raining outside and she didn't have a covered porch, so it was the best place they had to work.

Harper took a step back and shook her head. "The thought of using that thing scares me."

He smiled. "Okay, how about a hammer?" He held up the hammer.

She smiled. "That I can do."

Chapter Thirteen

Working alongside Nick was almost magical. Watching how he cut the pieces of wood and hammer them together to make two full walls was like watching an artist create a masterpiece. She didn't know exactly how he knew how to do everything, but by the time they were done for the night, there were two new walls made of lumber in the bathroom. One would separate what would be her new double sink area from the toilet and shower area, and the other was the wall for the shower, which would soon have tile on it.

Nick had surprised her by building a smaller wall with a top on it in the shower.

"This will be for the shower bench," he said when she asked.

She'd never dreamed she'd have a shower with a bench in it like his. She'd just hoped to have something big enough that she didn't bump her elbows on the sides while she washed her hair.

Then he'd gone one step further and told her that he could build a shower niche. She wasn't sure what that was, so she did a Google search. It was a box inside the wall to hold her shampoo and soap bottles.

"We made good progress today," he said, standing back as he dusted off his hands.

"We? I basically stood back and handed you tools and kept your iced tea glass full," she replied as she leaned on the doorframe.

"A very important job." Nick chuckled. "How early can we be here tomorrow?" he asked, motioning to Blue, who was snuggled up next to Lucy on her dog bed.

"How early do you want to be here?" she threw back at him.

He smiled. "I'll bring donuts and coffee." He snapped his fingers, and Blue groaned but got up from the bed and followed him to the front door.

She didn't know what she had expected as a goodbye. It was slightly shocking when he stopped at the door, pulled her into his arms, and kissed her until she forgot her name.

Before she could recover, he and his dog were gone.

Lucy whined at her feet, shaking Harper out of the stupor that kiss had caused.

"They'll be back tomorrow," she told Lucy as the truck's taillights disappeared down the driveway.

Covering her lips with her fingers, she stood in the door and watched the rain for a few moments.

She'd pulled away from him for a reason. It was for the best. She had to focus on Hailey's safety. On securing a future here for her sister. Even if that meant fighting for it.

There was a reason she'd started construction on the bathroom. She wanted Hailey to have a real home. Someplace she loved.

Sure, a little part of it was for herself too, but Hailey was the one who complained constantly about only having one small bathroom.

She'd give anything for her sister. She had done so her entire life.

The more she thought about things, the more positive she became that she wasn't going to let herself be run out of Pride. There was no way she was going to let her past push her out of the one and only place she and Hailey had ever felt like they belonged.

Watching the rain now, she could feel pride and comfort swell inside her for what they'd built here. She'd never felt anything like that anywhere else.

When her stomach growled, she made herself and Lucy dinner and then watched television with the dog snuggled up against her feet.

The next morning, she opened the door to help Nick carry in a huge box of sweets from his aunt's bakery.

They sat at her dining room table and downed their coffee and enjoyed a variety of donuts, muffins, and kolaches.

There was so much food there that she was sure they'd have plenty for lunch.

When Hailey came in, she sat down and ate with them and then disappeared back into her room to get ready for work later that day.

When Harper suggested she lend a hand, Hailey laughed and walked out of the room. "You made the mess, you clean it up," she called over her shoulder.

"Where do we start today?" Harper asked Nick when they were alone.

"Today, we put up the tile backer, do a little wiring, and some plumbing for the sinks. If all goes well, we can have the sinks in and usable by the time we're done."

"Then let's get to work." She clapped her hands and had both dogs bouncing around happily.

This time, she was more hands-on. She helped Nick lift the huge sheets of backing board for the tile into place and held them while he screwed them into the walls he'd built yesterday.

Within hours, the shower was looking like a real shower, minus the tile. Nick had her sit on the bench a few times to make sure it was the right height, then they found the best place for the niche. She took Hailey's tallest shampoo bottle and set it in there to make sure it was tall enough.

She had to admit, she was having a blast.

When they started working on the vanity, the work slowed to a crawl.

She had to keep flipping off the electric so Nick could change out old wiring with new and attach the new lights they had purchased for above the two sink mirrors.

"I wanted to ask you about the photographs on the walls. Were those your uncle's doing?" he asked when they broke for lunch. He motioned to the photo of an old barn just down the road that she'd taken one rainy morning.

"No, I took those. I found an old camera of my uncle's and learned how to develop film," she answered between bites of her sandwich.

"You... you took them and developed them yourself?" he asked, sounding surprised.

"Yeah. I turned what used to be a shop area in the carport into my darkroom." She scratched Blue's head as he begged at her feet.

"Can I see?"

"Sure." She got up to take her plate to the sink.

Nick followed her outside to the carport area where her

car and the back of his Jeep sat under the protection from the rain that had yet to stop since midday yesterday.

She opened the door and turned on the light, and he followed her into the small space.

She had three strings tied up over an old work bench. Her latest photos hung on them.

She reached up and started gathering them, but Nick stopped her so he could examine each of them carefully.

She and Lucy had taken a hike one foggy morning, and she'd thankfully taken her camera with her.

"This shot is amazing." Nick turned a photo around, and she smiled at the image of a large buck standing between a row of trees in the mist and looking at her.

"I thought he was going to charge me. Thankfully, Lucy didn't bark at him and he turned and walked away. We had a moment and then he was gone." She sighed and enjoyed the memory playing in her head.

"I want this," he said, suddenly. "A copy. Can you blow it up?"

She was surprised and took the image from him.

Yeah, it was good. You could see the mist swirling around the buck and see his breath in the cool morning air. His eyes were gentle. Searching.

"I hadn't realized it turned out so good," she said under her breath.

"It's amazing. All of these are." He held up another one of the buck standing on top of the hill, walking away from her. Here, he was nothing more than a shadow in the mist. "I want a copy of this one too."

She chuckled. "After all the work you've done in the past two days, you can have whichever of my pictures you want."

Nick's head jerked towards hers and then he smiled

slowly. "Promise?" He raised his eyebrows.

She felt her face heat and then she smiled. "Isn't that breaking a law or something? Sending nude photos?"

He set down the stack of photos he'd been looking through and was beside her in an instant. When he reached for her, she went into his arms.

"In some states, but thankfully not Oregon." He leaned down and kissed her. "Trust me. I am the law."

She laughed and wrapped her arms around his shoulders. "Does that line ever work for you?"

He smiled. "I'll let you know." He kissed her again, this time softer, a quick brush against her lips. "Seriously, you could sell some of these." He turned back to the stack of photos. "Can I take theses?"

"Sure, I have the negatives." She motioned to the small file cabinet she kept all of her negatives in, ordered by date for ease.

"How did you learn how to develop film? I mean, it's sort of a dying art. Everything is digital now." He tucked the photos into a large envelope that she handed him.

"I watched a few videos. It took a few times to get it right. I think I ruined about ten rolls of photos of my feet before I finally got it right," she joked.

"How long have you been doing this? The photography, the developing?" he asked.

"Just over a year. I started the month after we moved here."

"But you took pictures before? Got some training somewhere?" he asked with a frown.

"No." She didn't want to tell him that she'd never really seen a camera before getting her cell phone the year after she and Hailey had left Georgia. "We should get back to work," she suggested and they went back inside after Nick put the envelope of photos into his Jeep. He'd obviously returned his father's truck the night before.

Harper had seen other kids' cell phones when they were younger. And she had her picture taken on picture day at school. But never had she snapped a photo before that first day when she'd loaded the roll of film into her uncle's old camera.

Thankfully, the camera had come with a carry bag, a few different lenses, and the instruction book.

After she'd gotten the job at the restaurant, she'd used a portion of her first few paychecks to buy rolls of film. The rest of her money had gone to reconnecting the electric and paying the back taxes on the cabin.

Thankfully, when they'd gone into the county clerk's offices, they hadn't been questioned too intently and had set up payment plans. It helped that they had brought along the letter that had been delivered to their mother's mailbox showing she had gained possession of the property along with a copy of her death certificate, which Harper had printed out at the library.

When she'd found the paperwork, she'd assumed that Fred didn't know about the property. It was the reason they'd headed there in the first place. She'd believed they'd be safe there, at least from Fred.

Harper felt a shiver race down her back.

"Problems?" Nick asked and glanced up at her.

He was lying on his back under her new sink, connecting the plumbing while she held the light for him. Obviously, the light had shifted when she'd gotten lost in her own thoughts.

"No." She aimed the flashlight beam where he'd asked her to hold it. "Sorry." She tried to focus on anything but her past.

They had already hung the drywall on the new wall separating the two sections. Nick had sprayed it with a can of texture and now it looked almost identical to the rest of the walls in the room and the house. Nick said she could start painting in an hour or two after the texture dried.

"Why photographs?" he asked as he got back to work.

"I found the camera and decided to try it."

"You have a good eye. That sort of talent usually takes training," he said. She could tell he was making small talk and since the topic wasn't about her past, she figured she could open up to him about this at least.

"I've always found beauty in nature. When I was younger, Hailey and I would spend a lot of time outside. There was this creek by our place, and we'd hang out there. It was so beautiful, I always wished I could take an image of it with me when I left." She sighed and realized the light was slipping again and straightened it. "What about you? You obviously liked music lessons enough to continue playing."

"Sure. Piano was fun once I started learning some of my favorite songs instead of that crap that they make you practice when you're a kid. I swear I never want to hear 'Row, Row, Row Your Boat' or 'Twinkle, Twinkle, Little Star' again. He chuckled and then grunted as he tightened the pipe with the wrench. "Then I picked up the guitar and fell in love. I even took one with me when I went overseas." He scooted out from under the sink. "All done." He sat up and turned on the faucet. Water streamed out of it perfectly. He glanced under the sink and smiled. "She's holding." He moved over to start on the other sink.

She scooted over and held the light in the same place as she had on the other sink.

"This is all just so amazing. I never thought I'd have my

very own sink. Hailey is going to flip when this is all done," she said, letting the excitement roll off her.

"You two have a different a relationship than Kate and I," he said, as he started to work.

"How so?" she asked with a slight frown.

"Don't get me wrong, Kate and I are close. I'd kill for her, but..."

Harper's hearing all of a sudden dulled and the rest of what Nick said was muffled. She took several deep breaths.

"Hey." Suddenly he was sitting beside her, her shoulders in his hands. "Are you okay?" Worry laced his voice and filled his eyes.

She nodded, not trusting her voice.

"Breathe," he said slowly, and she focused on his eyes and calm voice until she was back under control.

"Want to talk about it?" he asked when the panic attack was over. She shook her head, but he arched his eyebrows.

"It's just... For as long as I can remember, it was just us two. Our mother was..." She swallowed.

"Addiction can be very time-consuming and costly to those around it," he broke in when she didn't continue.

Harper nodded. "I stepped up. If I hadn't, Harper wouldn't..." She stopped, remembering the last day they'd lived under the decrepit roof in the dirty building they had called home all of their lives.

She hadn't realized tears were rolling down her cheeks until Nick gently wiped them away with his thumb.

"It must have been so hard for you. You're a sister and a mother to Hailey," he said softly.

She swallowed hard and then nodded. The weight on her chest lifted slightly at his words.

"Yes," she agreed. "Everything I've ever done was for her. Like you said..." Her eyes met his. "I'd kill for her."

Chapter Fourteen

As much as he wanted to show emotion at Harper's words, he held still and waited.

He'd witnessed a full-blown panic attack before. Several times, actually. He'd never expected her to have one seemingly out of the blue.

It wasn't until she repeated his words back to him that he finally understood.

This was why she was running. This was why she was afraid of the law.

Harper had protected Hailey somehow and, in the process, had either hurt someone or killed someone.

Was she really worried he would think differently of her if he knew?

The truth was written all over her face.

Why had she revealed this now? Maybe it was because she'd just had a few moments of being unable to hide anything during her panic attack.

Whatever the reason, what he did next would mean everything.

He pulled her into his arms and held onto her.

"I'm here," he whispered into her hair. "I'm not going anywhere."

They were sitting on her bathroom floor, covered in a layer of dust and dirt, and she had finally opened up to him. For the first time, he had seen through her façade. He'd seen the truth about her past, whether or not she had meant to show him.

"Wow, this looks amazing," Hailey said from the doorway, causing Harper to jump away from Nick.

Before her sister could see, Harper wiped her eyes dry and busied herself by standing up and dusting off her jeans while she recovered.

"Thanks, we're not done yet," Nick said with a smile. "But at least you can now brush your teeth in your own sinks." He bent under the sink and finished connecting the drains. Then he turned on the faucet and smiled.

When he stood up, Hailey was hugging Harper.

"Thank you. I had no idea it could look like this," she said before letting Harper go to walk through the new shower area.

"We're going to start tiling tomorrow," Harper added, sounding excited again. "Here are the tiles we picked out."

For the next half hour, Harper told Hailey everything they had planned.

Hailey changed into a worn pair of jeans and a T-shirt and helped them for the next hour.

While he finished up with the plumbing and secured the new vanity to the wall, the sisters started painting the new walls a soft cream color.

"This is the last thing I can do tonight," he said when Harper and Hailey's conversation broke for a moment. "I'm going to head out. I'll be back in the morning and we can start on the tile."

"How long will that take?" Hailey asked. "I'm dying for a shower in this." She tapped the new shower wall.

"About two more days. You can shower on the third day."

Hailey surprised him by giving him a hug. "Thanks," she said, pulling away suddenly. "Really."

He nodded, then glanced over at Harper, who avoided his gaze.

"Blue," he said as he stepped out of the room. His dog fell in step with him as he grabbed his coat and headed outside.

"Nick?" Harper called out to him. He stopped just inside the doorway as she rushed towards him.

"Thank you." She lifted on her toes to kiss him briefly.

He nodded and, without another word, turned and left.

The entire drive home, he thought about her words. The meaning hidden behind her eyes.

Had she really killed someone?

She'd mentioned being afraid of Heidi and of Fred. He assumed that Heidi was her mother. Was Fred their father? Were either of them still alive?

He itched to do a background check on her. It wouldn't be hard. Next time he was on shift he could simply punch her name into the system.

If she had an Oregon driver's license, her information would be in there.

Any past tickets or arrests would show up.

He knew that they had come from Georgia. Harper had mentioned that they had grown up in a small town in the state. That they were from the south was obvious in their slight southern accents as well.

He and Blue got home almost an hour before sunset, so

he took the dog to walk on the beach and get some exercise while he weighed his options.

January along the Oregon coast was beautiful. All of the tourists were gone or tucked away out of the cooler weather.

The heavier rain had finally stopped, but it was misting enough that his hair was soaked by the time they hit the wet sand.

Blue took off running down the beach and grabbed the first big stick he found and carried it with him as he dodged the waves and sniffed the sand for crabs.

Nick sat down at one of his favorite thinking spots, a huge driftwood log that had rolled in the previous spring, and thought.

He'd said the words a hundred times in his life.

I'd kill for my family. I'd protect someone I love with my life.

When he'd joined the army, he'd done just that for his team. He hadn't gone into the military as a MP. Still, he'd been thankful he'd decided to pursue law enforcement.

Having to arrest one of the guys he'd been in basic training with had been tough. Seeing the destruction the man had caused his family had been tougher.

Since then, Nick hadn't had to deal with spousal abuse to that extent again, though he knew that, even in Pride, terrible things like that existed.

He'd broken up arguments, seen neglected children, dealt with drunk-and-disorderly calls.

But not once had he had to show up and cuff a man covered in his wife's and children's blood. Closing his eyes, he tried to shake those images from his mind.

PTSD did strange things to the mind. Mike Rowden's mind had snapped, and his wife and two young twin daughters had paid the ultimate price for it.

Suddenly, a very large, very wet stick dropped in his lap. He opened his eyes and smiled down at Blue, who sat directly in front of him, waiting for a game of fetch.

"You are happiness," he told Blue, then he threw his stick and laughed as the dog fell over his feet as he ran to catch it.

His mood was lighter the following day when he showed up at Harper's place with breakfast sandwiches and fresh coffee.

As with the previous two days, Blue and Lucy were thrilled to see one another.

"I think they miss each another every time you leave." Harper laughed as the dogs raced around the kitchen.

Since Hailey was off work that day, she helped them start the tile in the shower area. While he was the only one cutting the tiles and working with the mud, the sisters helped him by handing him the tiles and determining the patterns they wanted.

They had picked small octangle tiles for the flooring and, by his count, there was enough of it left over to do the back walls of the niche. The larger tiles would go on the walls and the bench, along with the matching bullnose tiles that fit the outer corners.

This was a job he loved to do. When it had been his place and his shower, he'd been frustrated at the time it had taken him to complete the task because he'd only had a few hours each night to work on it. Luckily, he had another shower down the hallway that he could use while his was under construction.

Knowing that the sisters only had the one shower did put some pressure on him. Still, the three of them worked fast enough that shortly after lunchtime all the tiles were finally on the walls with spacers between them.

"It will have to dry overnight as it is. Tomorrow we can grout," he told them. "If you need, you both are welcome to use the guest shower at my place."

"Are we that ripe?" Hailey joked, causing him to chuckle.

"No, just offering."

"Thanks, but I've been using the showers at the club." She glanced down at her watch. "I have another session with Reece in an hour. I'll get my things and head down early so I don't knock him out with my stench." Hailey laughed as she left the kitchen.

"How about you?" he asked Harper.

She bit her bottom lip and then sighed. "Yes, fine, I stink and I'd love a shower. I don't think I can wait two more days either. I'll get a bag of my things and meet you over at your place."

He tried to hide his smile by leaning down and petting Lucy and Blue. Then he headed back home.

He had every intention of convincing her to stick around after the shower long enough to talk for a few hours, have dinner, and possibly even watch a movie or go for a walk with the dogs. Hell, what he really wanted to do was spend a few hours necking on the sofa. He was perfectly fine with any of those options.

Before she arrived, he put a few dishes away that were drying on the rack in the sink.

Normally, he made sure everything was perfect before he left his place. He supposed it was something left over from his military days. But he'd also grown up in a neat and tidy home and enjoyed coming home to a clean house.

He wasn't annoying about it or anything. He'd dated a girl in high school who was a borderline slob. It hadn't bothered him at first. Then he'd gotten into her car one time and had stepped on a slice of moldy pizza on the floorboard of her car.

She'd giggled off the incident, and a week later he'd broken things off.

Harper and Hailey's place was older and outdated, but it was just as tidy as his place. That told him a lot about the sisters.

He knew by Harper's stories that they hadn't grown up with much. What they did have, they treasured and took care of.

Whatever Harper had or hadn't done in her past to protect her sister, there was no doubt in his mind that she wasn't a bad person.

When Harper knocked on the door, Blue rushed to greet her and Lucy.

"Hey." He opened the door wide for them.

"I really appreciate this," Harper said, shifting a backpack on her shoulder.

"I should have offered it sooner," he admitted as he shut the door behind them.

"I can use the one in the basement," she said as the dogs chased one another. "They just saw each other less than fifteen minutes ago." She laughed when they almost knocked her over.

"Yeah, I think they each get lonely when the other isn't around. Go, shower. I'm going to head up and do the same."

She frowned as she headed towards the stairs. "That won't eat up the hot water, will it?"

"No, there's plenty. Shower for as long as you want." He went up the stairs.

While he showered, all he could think about was her, two floors below him, naked and wet.

He pulled on a pair of clean clothes when he was done and went downstairs to make something to eat.

When Harper came upstairs, freshly showered and in a clean pair of jeans and a sweatshirt, he had two steaks, baked potatoes, green beans, and rolls warming in the oven and an opened bottle of wine on the table.

"Hungry?" he asked as she set her bag down near the door.

"I wasn't until I smelled all that." She motioned to the table. "Wow, it smells amazing. How did you cook all this so quickly?"

He laughed. "You took a long shower."

She groaned. "I could spend another hour there. It felt so good." She wrapped her arms around herself as she sat down. He took the spot next to her and poured her a glass of wine.

"This isn't some ploy to get me to stay the night, is it?" she asked, the glass to her lips.

"Would it work?" he asked.

She smiled before she took a sip. "Maybe." Then her smile slipped, and he knew she was thinking about her sister.

"Just what do you expect you could do to protect her that she can't do herself?" he asked as they ate. "If you're really worried, the two of you can stay here. I have three other bedrooms in this home and three fully working bathrooms."

She sighed and shook her head. "No, Hailey has made it very clear to me that she won't run and hide any longer."

"From?" he asked, taking a sip of his own wine.

He didn't think Harper was going to answer him at first. She took her time sipping her wine before answering. "My mother's boyfriend. Fred."

"Not your father?" he asked, noticing she hadn't touched her food yet.

Harper shook her head. "We... never knew who our fathers were."

"Fathers?" he asked. "Plural?"

"We assume. There are differences. My darker hair and eyes, Hailey's blue eyes and skin tone. I burn at the first sign of sunlight, while she turns a toasty brown."

"Okay." He figured there were probably other reasons besides looks that made them think they had different fathers, but he didn't think it was important at the moment.

"Fred started seeing my mother nine years ago. He was her dealer of this new drug she was into. It took her away from us physically and mentally, and led her down a spiral of addiction stronger than anything she'd been into before." Harper took another sip of her wine.

Her voice had taken on an automatic quality, as if she were telling a story that had happened to someone else. Maybe that allowed her to get through it. He'd seen it before in victims and knew better than to interrupt the disassociations. So, as she told her story, he sat quietly and listened to every word.

"We'd been attending school during the day when Fred first started hanging around. Then summer came and we were stuck with him for hours and hours during the day while he and Heidi got high. We escaped like we normally did when Heidi was vacant." She glanced in his direction. "That's the term we used for when she was high." He nodded his understanding. "Fred didn't do the same drugs he gave to Heidi. He stayed lucid most of the time. Smoked weed mainly. He didn't like us being too far from the house and, after the first few days of summer, he demanded we stay close." She took several more sips of wine before she started talking again. All the while he waited. Their food went untouched as she talked. "He started hitting me at first." She glanced in his direction for any reaction from him. He remained still.

He'd known it was something bad. He wanted to kill Fred. If the man ever came within arm's reach, he probably would. Still, he made a point not to react.

Harper picked up her wine glass again and rolled it slowly from side to side instead of taking another sip.

"Then he started sleeping over and things changed." She set her glass down and reached over to take his hand. He'd been gripping his steak knife so hard that his knuckles were turning white. Seeing this, he released his hold and flipped his fingers over to interlock them with hers. "I've never told anyone what I'm about to say. I'm not ashamed. I'm no longer a victim." She locked eyes with him.

He nodded again, not wanting to speak.

He knew she needed him to remain strong through the next part.

"That first night, I thought I'd done something wrong." She looked down at their hands. "The second and the many nights after, I knew without a doubt it wasn't my fault. Then six years ago"—her eyes jerked up to his—"he didn't come to my bed one night. When I woke up, Hailey was on my floor, crying."

His fingers jerked in her hands, and he walked over to the kitchen sink and stared blankly outside, unseeing.

Harper's arms wrapped around his waist. "I wanted to kill him," she said softly.

"Tell me you did kill him." He turned and wrapped his arms around her. "Tell me the bastard is dead."

Chapter Fifteen

Harper was shocked at Nick's response. Yesterday, she'd pretty much confessed to killing someone, and he'd looked at her as if he was trying to solve a puzzle.

Now, he was wishing that she had killed someone.

She shook her head against his chest. "No," she sighed. "I didn't kill Fred."

The night before, as she'd lay in bed, she'd decided to tell him everything. Whatever happened to her, it couldn't be worse than what she'd gone through years ago.

She knew that if she was locked up and dragged away from her sister, that Nick would be there to look after Hailey. That much was obvious. Nick and the rest of the town would take care of her. Hailey would be safe here. There was no doubt about that now.

Reece had even dropped by the house and ensured her that Hailey was doing amazing in his self-defense classes.

"Who?" he asked his arms tightening around her. "Then who is it you feel guilty of killing?"

She enjoyed the feeling of him holding her for a moment more before stepping back.

She leaned against the counter across from him.

"When everyone was asleep, later that night, I snuck into my mother's room. Fred was asleep on the floor. He hadn't even made it to the bed. His pants and boxers were still around his ankles." She closed her eyes as her stomach rolled. "Fred kept his stash of drugs under the mattress. Since he wasn't sleeping on it at the moment, it was easy to get to." She opened her eyes and looked out the window. The rain had stopped sometime the day before, but the sky outside was still gray as it grew darker. The view from Nick's window was nice enough that she felt some of the weight lift from her shoulders. "I knew where my mother hid the rat poison." Her eyes moved to Nick's. "But I didn't know which drugs were which, who took what. To me, it didn't matter. They both deserved it. They had been poisoning themselves for years." She shrugged and looked at her bare feet, at her pretty pink toenails, which Hailey had painted for her a few nights before while they were watching a movie.

"Your mother?" Nick asked, gaining her attention again.

She nodded. "By the time we woke, she was gone. She must have gotten into the stash after I left the room. Fred freaked. He grabbed his bag of drugs and left us there."

"Six years ago?" he asked. "You were..."

"Seventeen. Hailey was fifteen." She lifted her chin. "Instead of calling the police, as we'd been warned our entire lives never to do, we packed our bags and ran."

"You've been running ever since?" he asked, standing stiff against the counter across from her.

"Yes." She straightened her shoulders. "Now that I've confessed, are you going to arrest me?"

Nick surprised her by shaking his head from side to side almost immediately.

"You've confessed to adding poison to the drugs. There's no proof your mother ever took them. She could have been dead already when you walked into the room. She could have OD'd long before Fred... before..."

She nodded. "We hid for the first year, until after my eighteenth birthday, so afraid that we'd be found and separated by the system we'd been warned about our entire lives. We were living in a small weekly hotel just outside of Atlanta. I saved enough money to buy an old car by working at a strip club as a waitress, since I wasn't old enough to dance or work behind the bar." Her eyes met his. "One day, instead of going into work, I decided to go back and check the old house. The thought of my mother rotting in that place..." She visibly shivered, remembering the nightmares that she had and still did sometimes.

"What happened?"

"The place had burned down. Maybe it was Fred's doing, maybe it was natural. The mailbox, however, gave us the opportunity to move here. There was paperwork saying that my great-uncle had died and left my mother his cabin in a small town in Oregon." She smiled, then felt her anger grow. "We tried to find out if anyone had ever found her, seen the fire." She shook her head. "We found a death certificate online, so at least we knew that much." She sighed. "Then, one day while I was at work, there was Fred, sitting in a booth at the strip club with that damned grin on his face, as if he'd known just where I was this entire time."

"What did you do?" Nick asked, his eyes searching hers.

"I ran. We ran. We packed up and left town that night. It took us five years to make our way to the West Coast. Five very long years of jumping at shadows, hiding from the police, hiding from Fred. I worked shit jobs in hellholes to finally make enough to travel twenty-five hundred miles. I forced Hailey to finish her schooling. She walked into a college in Denver and passed her GED with flying colors." She smiled and felt pride swelling in her chest."

"Thanks to you," Nick said softly.

"I should have taken her away long before that night," she admitted.

Nick walked over and wrapped his arms around her. "Thank you for trusting me with this," he said into her hair.

She melted into his arms. "Thank you for not arresting me."

He chuckled and then leaned back. "If you want, I can look into what happened."

She frowned. "Would... It wouldn't raise any suspicions? If you did finally find out, that I was the cause of her death, what would happen?"

"Hey, let's deal with one thing at a time. If it turns out that your mother's cause of death was rat poison, then we'll deal with it. You were a minor at the time. Remember?" He ran his hands up and down her arms.

She nodded. "I'm tired..." She shook her head, remembering Hailey's words the night before. "We're tired of running. See what you can find out. Either way, I'll deal with it."

"We'll deal with it." He brushed his lips across hers. "Now, how about we heat up the food and eat it downstairs while we watch a movie?"

She smiled. "Sounds like a plan."

While he heated up their food again, she shot a text to Hailey and told her that she'd be home late.

"Don't worry, sis," Hailey replied quickly. "I'm going to be home late too."

Then they headed downstairs, each carrying a plate of food and their wine glasses. Nick had the rest of the bottle tucked under his arm.

They watched a romantic comedy and laughed through the entire thing as they ate. Her sides hurt from laughing, and her mood had lightened a million degrees by the end of the evening.

Nick turned off the movie when it was over and wrapped his arm around her.

"This is the part where I hope we spend the next hour on the sofa necking." He raised his eyebrows at her.

Smiling, she lifted up and straddled his hips. Her hands went into his hair as she ran her eyes over his face.

"I can do you one better," she said as she kissed him and moved over him. "I may not have been old enough to strip, but that didn't mean I didn't learn a few tricks." She raised her eyebrows back at him.

"Hell," Nick groaned as she slowly removed her shirt while gyrating on his hips. She could feel him grow hard against her and smiled.

"I hope you have some dollar bills ready," she purred as she tossed her shirt away.

"Hell," Nick groaned again, causing Harper to laugh.

She stood up and slowly gave him a private striptease show until she stood in front of him in just her bra and panties. Thankfully, she'd packed a sexy black lacy pair in hopes of getting naked with him again.

"Harper..." He started to stand up, but she pushed him back down with her foot against his chest as she smiled and slowly undid her bra.

"There's more." She held her bra out towards him with one finger. His eyes moved to her chest, and she saw them heat even further for her.

"Hell," he groaned once more.

She smiled. "Is that all you can say?"

"You're killing me," he growled, reaching for her. In one quick swoop, she was pinned under him on the sofa. The last black lace barrier was ripped aside as his mouth covered hers. He fumbled to unzip his jeans. Then he was gloriously inside her, and her legs wrapped around him, holding him deeper than she knew was possible.

"Mine," he whispered next to her ear when they lay tangled together, their skin and bodies cooling from the fast release.

"Mine," she replied back.

He shifted to look down at her. "I didn't hurt you, did I?"

She smiled as she shook her head. "Where's my dollar?" she teased.

He chuckled, his head resting against her breasts.

"Stay tonight?" he asked, without looking up.

Her smile slipped as her fingers stilled in his hair. "I can't."

He sighed and nodded. "Want another shower?"

She smiled. "I won't say no. My bag is upstairs though."

"You won't need it." In one quick move, he lifted her up in his arms and marched down the hallway to the guest bathroom she'd used earlier.

When they stood under the spray, wrapped around one another again, he stilled.

"I... shit. I didn't use protection." He searched her eyes.

She bit her lip and nodded. "I think I'm okay." She mentally calculated in her head and winced inwardly. "I can stop at the drugstore on my way home. Just in case."

"Don't," Nick surprised her by saying. "I mean, no, I

don't want..." He pulled her closer. "I'd love whatever the outcome is. No matter what."

She felt her heart skip.

"How did nothing happen. I mean..." He shook his head and turned off the water.

"You mean before?" she asked as he grabbed two towels and wrapped her in one then tied the other around his waist.

"Fred LeRoy may have been a perve, but he was cautious. He always told me that if I told anyone, there was no evidence because he always used a condom. It was his word against some addict's slutty snot-nosed daughter." She held the towel tighter around her.

Nick nodded. "I'm sorry to bring that up again."

She shook her head. "No, it's okay. I opened up to you. It's fair game for us to talk about now. Like I said, I'm done running and hiding."

He walked over and wrapped his arms around her again. "You are so strong."

She laughed. "If that were true, I would have stopped jumping at shadows years ago."

"Hey, I still jump at shadows," he admitted as they made their way back to the other room to gather their clothes and dress.

"You don't jump at shadows." She sat on the sofa as she picked up her torn underwear.

"Sorry, I guess I owe you a new pair." He smiled and took them from her. "So I know what size to get you."

She laughed as he pulled on his jeans and shoved the torn material into his pocket.

"Thank you for tonight," she said once they were both dressed and gathering their empty plates and glasses. "For the showers." She smiled as he loaded the dishes into the dishwasher.

Once their hands were empty, he pulled her into his arms again. "Whatever happens, I'm here." He kissed the top of her head.

She nodded. "I don't think..." She shook her head. "It's the least of my worries."

"It shouldn't be a worry at all. Still..." He pulled back and searched her eyes. "What I feel for you is beyond what I can say. Nor do I want to tell you how I feel while standing in my kitchen." He smiled down at her. Then he kissed her.

She felt her heart skip as she held onto him. "I feel the same. I wouldn't have shared what I did had I not."

She felt him nod his head. Then her phone rang and she stepped back to answer it when she saw Hailey's number.

"Someone was in the house," Hailey screamed into the phone, and Harper's heart stopped.

Chapter Sixteen

Nick and Tom each made two rounds through the cabin. Then they headed outside and circled the building, but their flashlights could only shine so far into the woods that engulfed the small place.

There was no doubt that someone had been inside the cabin. All of the tiles that the three of them had spent hours putting up in the bathroom had been broken into tiny pieces and were lying all over the floor.

If he didn't know better, he would have assumed that a jealous lover had destroyed everything in a rage.

When they had arrived at the cabin, Hailey was standing on the porch under the bright light, still on the phone with Harper. Tom had arrived seconds before them in the cruiser, since he'd switched his on-call weeks with Nick.

They'd left the dogs at his place when they'd rushed out in a hurry. He'd taken the time to grab his personal firearm from the safe.

After getting there, Harper had rushed to hug her sister

and the pair sat in his warm Jeep while he and Tom searched the place.

Now that they had confirmed that whoever had done this was gone, it was time to tell the sisters about the destruction.

"No one is here now," he said, opening the door.

"Hailey said the bathroom tile was destroyed," Harper said, getting out of the Jeep.

He nodded. "Yeah, whoever did it went to town on the tile. They used my sledgehammer." He held in a groan as he thought of cleaning up the mess and starting all over. "At least they didn't touch the sinks or the walls."

Just then a truck skidded to a halt behind his Jeep, and Reece jumped out.

"Hailey?" Reece called out.

"Here." Hailey pushed past Harper and rushed into Reece's arms.

"Oh?" Harper said softly as she watched the pair. "That's new." She turned to Nick. "Did you know about that?"

He shook his head. "News to me."

Then they watched as the couple awkwardly pulled apart.

"Looks new to them too," he whispered.

"Are you okay?" Reece asked, looking towards the cabin. When he spotted Tom and Nick, he nodded a greeting in their direction.

"Yes, the place was empty when I got home," Hailey said, wrapping her arms around herself.

Reece walked over and shook Nick's and Tom's hands. "Anything disturbed?"

"Just the shower we worked hard to rebuild today." Hailey groaned. "Looks like we'll need to buy more tile."

"Grab your things," Harper told her. "Nick has offered to put us up at his place. Until we know who did this"—Harper glanced sideways at Nick and he understood she knew exactly who it was, as did he—"we're staying there."

"No, I can't." Hailey shook her head. "I won't run and hide. Besides, I refuse to be a third wheel in whatever this is." She motioned towards them.

"You could stay at my place," Reece said eagerly.

Hailey's eyebrows shot up. "Thanks, but no. I'm staying put."

"If she stays, so do I," Harper said.

"Then I'll camp out here," Reece said just as Nick opened his mouth to offer to do the same.

"Ditto," Nick added with a grin.

Both of the sisters sighed and then looked at one another. He could see Harper begging Hailey with her eyes.

"It may only be for a few nights," Tom jumped in. "You're welcome to come stay with Kate and I, but you'd have to sleep in a single bed," he added with a smile.

Hailey threw up her hands. "Fine." She turned to Reece. "I'll stay with you. I am not going to spend a night listening to them. Seeing them kiss once was enough for me." She rolled her eyes but had a smile on her lips.

He wanted to argue that his guest room was two whole floors below his and on the other side of the home, but seeing Reece's smile, he remained quiet.

"I'll help you get your things," Reece said and then followed Hailey inside.

"Want some help getting your things?" he asked Harper.

"No." She looked at Tom. "Just... make another sweep around the place and make sure he's gone."

When she disappeared inside, Tom turned to him.

"He?" Tom asked.

"Long story, but while we have the time, unlock the patrol car. I have a few names I want you to run for me."

Tom nodded and unlocked the car.

The first search was for Fred LeRoy out of Georgia. There were more than a dozen and since Nick had no clue as to the man's age, he had Tom print out the list for him.

The next search was Heidi Davis. This one was much easier.

Heidi Nichole Davis. Died six years ago, July tenth in Jasper County of an overdose of heroine. Time of death was marked as at or before eight o'clock p.m.

Which meant that her mother had already been gone long before Harper snuck into the room to poison the drugs.

Was that why Fred had been on the floor? Had he stumbled into the bedroom and, seeing her dead, he'd fallen asleep on the floor?

Nick's stomach turned.

"Is that their mother?" Tom asked. Nick nodded. "Is the Fred character their dad?"

"No, he was the mother's drug dealer and the scumbag that abused the girls." Nick glanced towards the house. "This stays under wraps. That last part anyway. Put an APB on Fred LeRoy. I don't want anyone with that name so much as stepping a foot in Pride again."

"I can check with a few of the hotels along the highway. I'm on shift for two more hours and it's a slow night."

"Thanks." Nick slapped his brother-in-law's shoulder just as Hailey and Reece stepped outside.

"I'll follow you," Hailey said firmly.

"Fine, but flash your lights if you think someone's following you," Reece told her.

Nick wondered what Hailey had told the man. He

wanted to ask, but just then Harper came outside with a bag.

Nick reached over and took it. "I need to grab some things for Lucy." She disappeared back inside.

"Oh, I forgot..." Hailey also disappeared inside.

Taking his chance, he turned to Reece.

"What has she told you?" Nick asked.

Reece shrugged. "Not much other than she and Harper have a stalker. It's why she's taking self-defense classes and Harper's taking shooting lessons from you."

This was news to him, but he played along and nodded. Yeah, that wasn't such a bad idea. He could at least teach Harper a few of the basic self-defense moves as well. Why in the hell hadn't he thought of it first?

"Keep her safe," he managed to say before the sisters stepped outside again. "If you see anything, call me or Tom."

"Got it." Reece smiled. "It's not the first time I've handled a stalker," he threw over his shoulder as he followed Hailey towards her car.

"Locked up?" he asked Harper as Reece's and Hailey's cars disappeared.

"Yeah." She turned towards him. "How did he get in?" she asked.

He was surprised and thought about it. "Did you leave a door open?"

Harper shook her head. "We were adamant about locking up."

"I'll have another look around." This time as he circled the home, he checked every window and door.

When he came back, he had his answer.

"The lock on the laundry room widow is busted. It slides open even if it's locked. I put a stick in it for now. That will stop him from getting in that way. Of course, if he really wants in, those are only single-paned windows. They break easily."

Harper closed her eyes and took a deep breath. "Right. Let's go." She turned and marched towards his Jeep.

As he drove, he filled her in on a few things.

"Tom will file a police report so you can let your insurance know. They might pay for the tiles to be replaced."

"Don't bother. I don't have insurance." She sighed as she looked out the window. "I'll just have to go with the plain white tiles this time."

He was quiet the rest of the way back to his place. When they parked, he helped her with her bag.

"I'm not sorry that you'll be staying with me," he said, setting her bag down inside as she loved on the dogs, who were as happy to see them as if they'd been gone for days instead of less than an hour.

"I thought I'd be tired after everything. Instead, I just want to punch something," she said, standing up.

He smiled. "I can help you out there." He took her hand and they made their way downstairs.

He opened his gym door and motioned to the punching bag. "Have at it."

She looked down at her clothes and then shrugged and walked over to the bag.

He stopped her from hitting it with her fist.

"First, do you know how to hit properly?" he asked.

She chuckled and held up her fist.

"Good, your thumb should always be on the outside like this." He tapped her fist. "Straight on. No wimpy wrists." He showed her slowly a few times. She mimicked his moves. "Good, now give it a go. Use your whole shoulder and arm. Don't just throw from your elbow."

He showed her the difference.

"Like this?" She followed his moves.

"Stand like so." He positioned her feet.

She followed and when he nodded, she threw a pretty solid punch and smiled. "More," she said, doing it again.

He stood back and watched her throw a couple more punches.

"Want gloves?" he asked after a moment.

She frowned down at her fists. "For now, I like the sting. I won't be wearing gloves when I punch Fred's teeth in." She smiled back at him.

"There's the warrior I knew was hiding in there." He walked over and kissed her.

"Now I'm tired," she admitted after a few minutes of hitting the bag.

"We can do more tomorrow if you want."

She nodded and then they headed back upstairs.

"What do you know about Fred?" he asked when they were sitting at the bar drinking water.

She narrowed her eyes. "His name, Fred LeRoy. Where he worked seven years ago when he met my mother—Iron Works Construction out of Atlanta. And every detail of each of his tattoos. At least the ones he had back then." He saw her shiver.

He took her hand in his before he pulled out the printout that Tom had given him.

The long receipt-like paper had the list of Fred LeRoys in the Atlanta area.

"Do you have a pen?" she asked, glancing up from the list.

He walked over to his junk drawer, which he had organized at the end of last year, and pulled out a pen.

He stood by while she scratched out almost half of the names.

"The rest are hard to narrow down. Any chance I can see the mug shots on these three?" she asked, showing him three circled names. "I know he was arrested for drug possession the month before we left. He spent a night in jail, and Heidi had to bail him out." She glanced up at him. "She sold her car to do so, which made her more reliant on him after. We had to ride the bus, which to be honest, was a blessing."

"Sure, tomorrow we can stop by the station on our way to pick up more tile. My dad has agreed to help us with the repairs. It should go faster." When he thought he saw her eyes watering, he pulled her into his arms. "Are you okay?"

She nodded. "I told myself to be strong. I'm pissed. Not scared."

He nodded. "I get that."

He felt his shirt get wet from her tears and just held onto her while she broke.

There really wasn't anything that he could say to comfort her. He could give her empty promises that he'd catch the guy and make him pay. But he knew that, unless the man messed up, the odds of that were slim.

If this was just a show of force and Fred wanted to scare the girls, he'd succeeded. He could be halfway back to Georgia by now.

The fact that the man went after the thing they'd spent a few days working on told him that he'd been watching them. He could be sitting outside the house now, watching, waiting. Or he could be outside of Reece's place.

Until he made a move, they were sitting ducks.

"I'm sorry," Harper said as she wiped her eyes with the sleeve of her sweatshirt.

"Don't be." He brushed a strand of her hair away from her face. "He wants you to be weak," he told her, and her chin rose an inch. "Be weak when he's not watching. Fight like hell and be freaking Wonder Woman if he comes for you or Hailey."

She nodded several times. "Tell me you have some chocolate ice cream in that big freezer of yours, and I'll agree never to leave here."

The sound of that warmed his entire body, and he smiled.

"Promise?" he joked.

She laughed. "Sure, why the hell not."

He tilted his head as he thought about his mistake earlier. He'd never gone without a condom. Never.

Part of his subconscious mind knew that he wanted to be with Harper. That he wanted to spend the rest of his life with her.

He didn't think he was the type to force someone's hand in staying with him. He doubted that was the reason he'd forgotten. Still, he *had* forgotten.

He'd been so caught up in being with her, his mind had just shut off.

Without saying anything more, he disappeared and got a quart of Rocky Road ice cream. He grabbed two bowls and spoons and set it all down on the bar top.

He dished them each a huge bowl, and they took the dessert into the living room and watched television.

After Harper fell asleep, he let the dogs out to do their business. When they came back, they had mud on their feet so he kept them in the laundry room. They immediately snuggled down for the night, content.

Then he went into the living room, picked up Harper,

and carried her up to the bedroom. She woke halfway up the stairs and held onto him.

"I'm so very glad I went with you to get a puppy." She sighed. "I've never felt this way about anyone before."

"Me either," he said, stopping at the top of the stairs to brush a kiss across her forehead.

"This whole town is amazing," she said as he set her down on the bed. She started pulling off her jeans and then removed her bra while he slid off his jeans.

They crawled into bed, and he pulled her close to his chest as she faced away. He wrapped his arms tightly around her.

"It's the reason Hailey and I are fighting instead of bolting. We love this place. We both want to stay. We used to have bug-out bags," she admitted, "just in case."

"But... you're staying," he asked, feeling his heart skip.

"Yes," she answered with a sigh.

"Good," he said. He felt her drift off to sleep.

He replayed their conversation, along with the events of the entire day, in his head as he lay there holding her. He thought all the way back to the first time he'd seen Harper. How she'd immediately spiked his interest. But her obvious fear had made him hesitate to ask her out right away.

When he finally drifted off to sleep, his dreams took him back to that night when he'd seen one of his friends covered in the blood of his family.

"Nick!" Harper shook him until he jolted awake.

"What?" He came off the bed, ready for a fight.

"You were having a nightmare," Harper said, looking up at him.

Every muscle in his body relaxed as he sat back down on the bed. He glanced at the clock and groaned.

The sun would be coming up in less than an hour.

Which meant there was zero chance of him falling back asleep now.

"Are you okay?" she asked, wrapping her arms around him.

"Yeah." He ran his hands over his face, already wishing for a do-over of the morning.

"Want to talk about it?" Harper asked.

He thought of telling her no, of trying to convince her to go back to sleep. But then he realized just how much she'd opened up to him in the past day.

He climbed into bed, pulled her into his arms, and started telling her the reason his dreams were haunted.

Chapter Seventeen

Listening to Nick's story earlier that morning put all of her worries and fears into perspective. She couldn't imagine seeing the things he had and not somehow breaking.

He was a lot stronger than most people in town knew. No wonder he didn't like talking about his time in the army. He'd witnessed so much blood and pain.

They ate a quick breakfast at his place and then headed to the police station. They would meet his dad at the hardware store afterwards.

It was strange walking into a police station. Her entire life she'd avoided cops, had been taught to fear them. She felt like she was a lamb walking into a lion's den the moment she stepped inside.

Nick took her hand and led her past the front desk area as he threw out a casual greeting to the woman sitting behind the desk.

A long hallway led back to a large room filled with cops, about ten of them. Some were sipping coffee, others talking on the phone or working on computers. All of them stopped and glanced up to greet Nick when he walked in.

"This is my desk." He motioned to a desk in the middle of the four rows of desks.

"Sit." He nodded towards the chair beside it as he took the seat behind the computer.

While they waited for his computer to boot up, she took several deep breaths and told herself she was being stupid for being afraid now. She knew every single cop in the room. She had served them drinks, chatted with them, laughed with them.

Even now, a lot of them greeted her or smiled in her direction. There was nothing to fear. Nothing.

"Okay," Nick said, turning the screen a little. "These are the three that you circled." He showed her the screen with images of three different men.

None of them were Fred. She shook her head. "No, none of those are him."

Nick nodded. "Okay, let's broaden our search." He typed for a few moments while she thought about the news that he'd given her the night before.

She hadn't killed her mother. In fact, her mother had been long gone when she'd tiptoed into the bedroom and mixed the rat poison with the white powder in the small bags. If anything, Fred was the one responsible for her mother's death.

Nick finished typing and then turned his screen once more and showed her a new row of images. Her heart skipped and then sank.

"No, none of these are him either." She sighed.

"Tell me about his tattoos," Nick asked. He typed while she told him about a few tattoos Fred had on his arms and hands.

This search narrowed it to one image. It wasn't Fred.

"Where in Atlanta was he?" Nick asked.

She shrugged. "He worked at Iron Works Construction out of Atlanta."

Nick typed. "There isn't a company called Iron Works Construction near Atlanta. Never has been." He sighed and leaned back. Then his phone buzzed. "My dad is at the hardware store."

She shrugged. "We tried."

"I work tomorrow. I'll have plenty of time to run a deeper search." He took her hand in his. "For now, let's just get your shower fixed."

She nodded and they headed back out of the station after talking briefly with Tom, who also promised her that he'd spend some time in his workday to help with the search.

Nick's dad greeted them in the tile row of the hardware store.

"Morning." Sean smiled at her. "How are you holding up?"

"Good. Thanks for agreeing to help out today." She felt slightly embarrassed for some reason. She'd never formally met the father of the man she was sleeping with, though technically she had known his parents for well over a year. She'd enjoyed chatting with them on several occasions.

"Well, I've got some good news for you," Sean said to her. "Steven here, who owns the hardware store, has graciously offered you the same tiles you chose a few days earlier at half the price to help out."

"Really?" She gasped. "Thank you." She turned to the older man, who smiled and nodded at her.

"We can't let hooligans win," Steven said as he turned and walked away to help someone else.

She knew it was going to stretch her budget for the month, but she decided it would be worth it to go all in instead of just getting the plain white tiles.

Listening to Nick and his father joke and laugh while they tore the rest of the tiles out of her shower lightened her mood and squashed any lingering fears she had.

Since she was mostly just in their way, she stepped out of the room and went to develop some of the pictures she'd taken a while back when she and Lucy had gone on a walk. She also figured she'd blow up the image of the buck that Nick wanted to hang over his fireplace.

Locking herself in her dark room was therapeutic. Watching the images appear on the paper still gave her a sense of wonder and awe.

While the larger image of the buck hung up to dry, she started working on the new roll from the week before.

She was on the third picture when she froze as the image appeared before her eyes.

He'd changed some. He was thicker. Stronger looking. He'd shaved his head completely and wore a thick black beard. That and the flannel coat, dark jeans, and hiking boots would have allowed him to fit in anywhere there were woods.

With shaky fingers, she finished the roll in hopes of a better picture.

When all of the film was hanging up to dry, she stepped outside to get Nick.

To her surprise, he and his father had already started hanging the new tiles they'd bought that morning at the hardware store.

"Do you have a minute?" she asked Nick. "I have something you should see." She held the one fuzzy image to her chest.

"Sure." Nick stood up and wiped his hands off.

"Lucy and I went on a walk last week. When it snowed. I don't know what day it was exactly, but..." She held the image out. "That is Fred."

Nick tensed and then took the image from her.

"I didn't see him. When we were out walking. I didn't even know I'd gotten a picture of him until just now when I developed the roll. This is the only picture I got of him. He must have followed us." She felt her fear spike.

Nick wrapped his arms around her as he held the image up for his father to take.

"Tell me this will help find him," she said into Nick's chest. "He's been watching us for a while."

"Yeah, it'll help," he assured her.

"Why don't we head down to Baked for some pizza and a break?" Sean suggested. "Nick can swing this by the office to help Tom in his search."

"Sounds like a plan," Nick agreed. "We can let the mud dry and maybe grout when we get back. You should have a completed shower by tomorrow," he added with a smile.

While she and Sean sat in Baked waiting for Hailey to deliver their food, Nick ran down the street to the station to drop off the photo with Tom.

Hailey didn't have much time to chat, and Harper didn't want to cause her sister to worry by telling her that Fred had been sneaking around their place for weeks.

She was happy to see Reece sitting in a corner booth, working on his laptop. Outside of his boxing career, she wasn't quite sure what the man did.

She knew that Reece had recently purchased a house just outside of town up on the hillside that overlooked Pride.

Every now and then Reece would glance up and watch

Hailey and then glance towards her and nod, as if saying, "Yeah, I've got you covered."

She appreciated him even more and, even though she barely knew the guy, she trusted him with her sister's safety.

Nick had told her that he, Tom, and Reece had grown up together. She was pretty sure Nick was just trying to get her to relax about not constantly watching over her sister.

When Nick finally returned, he sat next to her and wrapped his arm around her shoulders.

"Tom is on it," he assured her. "Where's our food?" He glanced towards the back.

"Hailey was keeping it warm until you returned." She waved towards her sister, who brought out their pizza and refilled her soda.

While they ate, it was obvious to Harper that they avoided talking about Fred and what had happened. Instead, the father-son duo talked about everything else. The town. The past holiday seasons. The coming Valentine's celebrations.

"Valentine's?" She focused on the conversation again.

"Yeah, it's less than a week away." Nick smiled. "I was going to ask you to be my Valentine date." He took her hand and kissed it.

"Gross," Hailey said as she refilled Sean's tea.

"What did you have in mind?" she asked Nick, ignoring her sister.

"I'll think of something." Nick smiled back at her. "When I'm not sitting across from my father while your sister stands over us."

She laughed and nodded.

When they returned to the house, she was relieved that nothing had been messed with. Maybe Fred had left town? Maybe he'd only destroyed the bathroom to scare them.

But why would he come all this way just to scare them? They were nothing to him. Just the daughters of a woman he'd killed with drugs. Two young girls he'd tortured years ago.

All this time, they hadn't really been running from him. Harper had believed for so long that she'd killed her mother and somehow the police would find out and lock her up.

Those first years on the road, she'd feared that Hailey would be taken from her. After all, her sister had been a minor until three years ago.

Still, after her run-in with Fred at the club all those years ago, the fear of seeing him again played in her mind. She'd never imagined something like this though.

The man traveling across the country to do petty things such as destroy their property. Why? Control?

Surely, he knew that the sisters had grown up and outgrown the fear he used to instill in them when they'd been under his control.

While Nick and his father returned to grouting the tile, she cleaned the rest of the house, a nervous habit she'd gained shortly after she and Hailey had moved into the cabin.

They'd never had control of anything growing up. The small house they'd been raised in had always been dirty. Junk piled up everywhere. She doubted that their mother had ever swept or used a vacuum cleaner.

Because of this, both Hailey and Harper had become neat freaks when they'd moved out on their own. Seeing Nick's place that first day, so tidy and organized, had been a huge relief.

There were so many things that drew her to Nick. Besides his kindness and the fact that he was the best-looking man she'd ever seen, they seemed to have the same sense of humor. They liked the same style of movies and music and even food.

She kept trying to talk herself out of feeling so much for him, but by the end of the day, when she stood looking at her perfect new shower, she had to face facts. She was in love with Nick. Full-blown love.

Chapter Eighteen

The day after he'd finished rebuilding Harper's shower, Nick sat at his desk in the station and scrolled through mug shot after mug shot.

He'd widened his search to beyond Georgia. Still, he hadn't come across any men named Fred LeRoy that resembled the image Harper had taken of the man stalking them.

During his lunch break, he went down to the Golden Oar and sat at the bar to eat lunch with Harper while she worked.

It was during his break that he came up with another idea. Unfortunately, he had a call afterward about a four-car wreck on the highway that kept him out of the office until his shift ended.

Since Harper wasn't due to get off work for another hour, he figured he'd swing by the station and run a few more searches.

When he walked in, Aiden was the only one in the office, and he was on the phone with his door shut.

He booted up his computer and punched in "Heidi

Davis" and re-read everything the state of Georgia had on the woman.

When her charred body had been found in the wreckage of her home, it had been assumed that she had died of natural causes. Then the autopsy came back with the overdose and time of death, which had been a full two days before her body had been found. Amongst the wreckage there had been plenty of drug paraphernalia which, along with her lengthy rap sheet, had closed the case quickly.

No one had even looked for the woman's two underage daughters at that point. There was actually no mention of them. Nor of Fred, a boyfriend, or a drug dealer who had been living with them.

Switching over from the official channels, he searched for news articles. Surely, there must have been something about the fire in the small town's newspaper.

When all he found was a simple paragraph or two about Heidi Davis's death in the fire, he almost gave up.

There was an image of the burned building along with a grainy photo of Harper and Hailey's mother.

Instantly, he could see slight resemblances between the daughters and the woman. The image was obviously an old photo. Heidi Davis looked young, around seventeen or eighteen. She looked more like Hailey than she did Harper. In the photo, she looked high, even back then.

He was about to turn off his machine and call it a night when he decided to search for Fred and the place Harper mentioned he'd worked, Iron Works.

Instead of typing in Iron Works Construction, he just put in Iron Works and got a few links to a strip club called Iron Works just outside of Atlanta.

He clicked on the business profile of the business and was shocked to see Fred's image as the business owner.

"Son of a..." He leaned forward and scanned the information.

Fredrick Leeroy, was a forty-eight-year-old businessman who had purchased the very successful Iron Works Strip Club six years ago. The man had worked at the club as a bouncer for the two years prior to purchasing the business.

So how did a low-life drug dealer manage to come up with enough money to buy a successful strip club shortly after Harper's mother died?

Since he had the man's real name now, he ran a search and came up with a very long rap sheet. He printed a copy and then ran another internet search to find out all he could on the man.

The more he looked into the man, the more disgusted and pissed off he became.

Seeing that Aiden was still in his office, he knocked on the door.

"Yeah," Aiden called out.

"Hey, boss," Nick said as he opened the door.

"What are you still doing here?" Aiden glanced at his watch and sighed. "What am I still doing here?" He chuckled.

"This is Fred." He walked over and set a copy of the printout on Aiden's desk.

Aiden glanced over the paper and then nodded. "Okay, I'll put out an APB."

"There's more." He set the next paper down. "Months before Heidi Davis died of an overdose, Fred purchased a large life insurance policy on her and her two daughters, along with insurance on their property, which had been handed down to Heidi Davis from her folks. To the tune of half a million dollars. When Heidi Davis died, the policy paid out on her and the property."

"Okay, so Fred got the payout," Aiden said with a shrug. "What does he want with the sisters?"

"He tried to report that both of the girls were killed in the blaze. The insurance company disagreed, claiming that he had no proof of the girl's demise."

"Shit," Aiden sighed. "You think he's come back to finish the job?"

Nick shrugged. "I've already contacted the insurance company. Well, I left them a message and sent them a report, at any rate. I'm curious if he still is holding the policy. Something tells me the insurance company wouldn't renew something like that after what he pulled."

"That's a shaky reason to come across the country and kill. In hopes of getting a payout from a policy he's been paying into for the past... how many years?"

"Six," he supplied. "I agree." He thought about telling Aiden about the abuse the sisters had suffered at the man's hands. "There are other reasons, ones I'm not at liberty to go into with you just yet."

Aiden met his eyes and a look of understanding crossed between them. Then he stood up and stretched. "Okay, so we add some extra protection on the sisters." Aiden smiled. "Rumor has it you've already got that covered for Harper."

Nick smiled and nodded. "Hailey is staying with Reece currently."

Aiden nodded. "Tell me what you need."

"For now, the APB will have to do. Something tells me the man hasn't strayed far. He's playing a petty game with them right now. Toying with them. From what I've heard and from looking at his rap sheet, he likes to push around anyone weaker than him."

Always My Love

Nick glanced down at the man in the photos. Your average meathead gym rat, with lots of muscles. He'd probably made the switch from recreational drugs to steroids, from the look of his latest mug shot.

"Okay, I'm heading home. Let me know if you need backup." Aiden slapped him on the shoulder.

After leaving the station, Nick swung by the Golden Oar to pick up Harper. Since she still had a few minutes of work left, he headed inside and sat at the bar.

He was happy when she didn't jump or look scared when she saw him in full uniform again. Even though she'd seen him dress and get ready for work earlier that morning, it was nice that instead of the worried look that had always filled her eyes when she saw him, she smiled.

"Evening, officer," Harper flirted as she leaned on the bar towards him.

"Ma'am." He winked at her. "Slow night?" He glanced around at the crowded bar area.

Harper chuckled. "Connie's taking over for me in a few." She rolled her shoulders. "Care for a tea?"

"Actually, I'll have a Coke."

"Want to order dinner here?" she offered as she filled a glass with the soda.

"Sure, what's the special tonight?" he asked, making himself comfortable.

Just then Harper glanced over his shoulder and her smile doubled. "Hailey and Reece just walked in." She waved at them.

The pair joined him at the bar.

"We saw your Jeep out front and thought we might join you for dinner," Hailey said. "When do you get off work?" she asked her sister.

"Five minutes," Harper answered after looking at her watch.

"Order us a couple of burgers. We'll grab a booth." Harper motioned to a booth in the bar area that had just become available.

"I'll have the same," he said.

Harper smiled and then turned and punched their orders into the computer.

"I have news," he said softly when she returned. Then he glanced at Hailey. "She deserves to hear it as well."

Harper bit her lip and then sighed. "Okay, you can tell us." She motioned and then Connie stepped behind the bar.

"Go on. Your family is here. I've got this," Connie said as she went to take someone's order.

"Thanks." Harper gathered her coat and purse from behind the bar.

When they sat down across from Hailey and Reece, Harper turned to him.

"Nick has news he wants us to hear." Harper shifted to sit almost sideways in the booth.

"We found Fred." He pulled out the printout and laid it on the table. While he filled the three of them in on what he'd found, he watched Harper's expressions, which mirrored those on Hailey's face.

Both sisters were determined and angry instead of afraid. A good sign.

By the time their food arrived, the four of them were in deep conversation, speculating as to what the man wanted from the sisters.

Neither of them mentioned the physical abuse in front of Reece, so he wasn't sure they wanted to share that much and kept that detail out of the conversation.

After their food arrived, the conversation turned to

Reece's boxing career. He was set to head out next month for a couple of big fights in Vegas and California.

"Is that how you afforded your home?" Harper asked.

"Harper!" Hailey hissed and kicked her sister under the table.

"What? I'm curious." She turned back to Reece and waited for his answer.

It was a lot like watching a mother ask her daughter's boyfriend what he wanted to be when he grew up, like his mother had done to Tom when he'd started dating Kate.

Nick couldn't help but smile as Reece answered nervously.

"My boxing career is taking off, but I still work for my dad's company. I've been programming games since I was ten."

"Right," Harper said. "I'd forgotten your dad owns... Modarth?"

Reece and Nick both chuckled. "Modark," they corrected at the same time.

Harper shrugged. "We didn't play video games growing up."

"Right." Reece smiled and then looked at Hailey.

Okay, so it was obvious Reece knew a little of the sisters' past at least.

For the rest of the meal, they talked about Pride gossip. It was as if everyone was done talking about Fred and the threat he was causing them.

Following Harper back to his place, he had a few moments to think. When they got home, it was after dark, and they sat out on his back deck area and watched the dogs play in the fenced yard.

"Tell me again that my sister is safe with Reece," Harper said again.

He must have assured her a dozen times already, but he answered her again.

"Yes." He wrapped his arms around her. "As safe as you are with me." He kissed her forehead and felt her relax.

"She's my world. I don't know what I'd do if anything happened to her." Harper leaned her head on his shoulder.

"Nothing will," he said, knowing he'd do all he could to protect both of them.

"How much money did he get?" she asked.

He'd neglected to state the amount earlier. All that mattered was that he'd turned around and had bought the strip club. Nick planned to find out how financially healthy the business was first thing in the morning.

"You know, I can't stay here forever," she said when they went back inside.

He wanted to ask why not, but then he remembered that she had a place of her own, where they had just fixed the shower, and kept his mouth shut.

"As soon as they figure out where Fred is, Lucy and I should probably go back home," she said as they cleaned off the dogs' muddy paws.

"What if you didn't?" he said. "I mean, Lucy and Blue miss each other whenever you leave."

The sides of Harper's mouth twitched. "Is that the only reason?"

He grinned. "My bed is far too big and cold when you're not in it."

"And?" she asked, wrapping her arms around him after setting the towel down.

"It's really hard to cook for one after you've been cooking for two," he pointed out.

She laughed and shook her head. "Nope, not good

enough reasons." She stood up suddenly and started to walk away.

He raced after her and grabbed her around the hips.

"I want you to stay," he whispered against her lips. "Please."

She smiled and said, "I'll think about it." She nudged him away, but the fact that she was smiling up at him assured him that the answer, when she wanted to tell him, would be yes.

Chapter Nineteen

Valentine's Day was quickly approaching and Nick had yet to tell her his plans. She'd gotten the night off at his request. Whenever she asked him what they were going to do, he avoided answering her by distracting her with sex or other topics.

Not that she complained. She'd never had anyone surprise her with something nice before. Then again, she'd never officially had a boyfriend either. Nor a date on Valentine's Day.

That thought had put her in a sheer panic one afternoon when she realized that she didn't own a dress. Not a single one.

Most of her clothes were behind-the-bar attire or worn blue jeans and sweats for long walks. It ate at her so much that during her lunch break she headed down to the little boutique in town, Classy and Sassy.

She'd been inside the store a handful of times since moving there, but since most of her money was spent on fixing up the cabin or developing her photos or buying rolls of film, she hadn't purchased anything other than a few smaller items.

Definitely not a dress. She'd had no occasions to wear a dress. Until now.

She knew the owners, Lilly and Riley, very well. The cousins and their husbands, twins Corey and Carter, owned Baked.

Today, Lilly was leaning behind the counter, staring at the computer screen, while Riley was busy helping another customer.

When Harper walked in, Lilly glanced up at her and smiled.

"Hi, Harper." She straightened and walked around the counter. "What brings you in today?"

Harper held in a groan as she answered simply, "A dress. I need a dress for a Valentine's date."

Lilly smiled and then took her arm and started leading her around the store.

"I have just the one. You'll love it. It's supposed to be a little warmer for Friday and the weekend, so I think this will do nicely." She stopped at a rack and then pulled out a soft pink dress that looked like it would hit Harper mid-thigh. It had long puffy sleeves and a modest neckline.

"This dress with..."—Lilly walked over and picked up a pair of tan low-heeled boots—"these, and"—she grabbed a long knit sweater in soft cream—"this cardigan to ward off the chill after dark." Lilly held them up. "I've picked your sizes." She motioned to the dressing room. "Why don't you try them on?"

Harper had never tried on clothes in a boutique before, so it was still all new to her. Normally, she plucked jeans, T-shirts, sweaters, or whatever she needed off the rack and just paid and left.

She stepped into the dressing room. It felt strange pulling off her work clothes to put on the soft, pretty dress and shoes.

When she was dressed in the outfit, she looked at herself in the mirror and felt tears sting her eyes.

She looked like a girl. Scratch that, she looked like a woman.

"How does everything fit?" Lilly asked through the door.

"Good," she said, and then she cleared her throat as she wiped her eyes. "I'll take them."

"Well, come out and let us see!" Riley called out.

Harper fumbled with the door and then stepped out.

"Wow," Riley and Lilly said at the same time.

"You're going to knock Nick on his ass." Lilly smiled.

"You should wear your hair down. Maybe curl it a little if you can. I can never keep curls in my hair, not like Lilly can." Riley nudged her cousin's arm.

Harper nodded, not sure what to say next.

"Do you need a purse to go with the outfit?" Lilly asked, holding up a simple soft tan purse.

Harper had never owned a purse. She'd always carried around her backpack or a larger bag that she used as a purse. The thing Lilly held was small, dainty, girly. Like nothing Harper had ever owned in her life.

"I..." She thought about carting her big bag around wearing this outfit and then nodded. "Yes." She smiled. "I'll take it all."

Damn. She was going to have to work overtime next week just to pay for all these nice things for one dinner.

Still, she figured Nick was worth it. After all that he'd done for her and Hailey, he was so worth it.

With her new items wrapped in a hot pink Classy and

Sassy Bag, she made her way over to Baked to grab a slice of pizza.

Hailey happened to be taking her lunch at the same time and they sat at a table together.

"What's up between you and Reece?" Harper asked her sister.

Hailey's eyebrows rose slightly before she shrugged.

"I'm not sure." She frowned into her iced tea. "I mean, he's very protective. Almost brotherly." Hailey avoided her eyes.

Harper was surprised at this comment.

"He... he hasn't kissed you yet?" she asked.

She'd assumed, along with everyone else in town, that the two were an item. Like her and Nick.

Hailey shook her head.

Harper leaned closer and whispered, "What have you told him about... things." She glanced around.

Hailey shrugged. "A lot. Not everything, but a lot."

Harper took her sister's hand in her own. "I hope that one day you'll feel comfortable talking with someone like I am now."

"So Nick knows everything?" Hailey asked, her eyes searching Harper's.

"Yes," Harper answered softly.

"And... you're not in trouble?" Hailey whispered.

Harper smiled and shook her head. "No, even after I told him everything, he didn't even look at me differently. Besides, he's the one who found out that Heidi was already dead when I..." She dropped off. "He's gone out of his way to make me feel... different." She sighed and leaned back in the chair. "I think I'm in love," she admitted to her sister.

Hailey was quiet for a moment.

"I don't know if I'll ever be able to trust like that,"

Hailey said, looking down as she swirled her straw in her tea. "To tell someone my biggest secret. My biggest shame."

Harper reached across the table and gripped Hailey's hand.

"Nothing you did was shameful," she asserted. "You did nothing wrong. Neither of us did."

Hailey's eyes started to tear up, but she nodded slightly.

Harper could tell that her sister struggled to believe it.

"Are you okay staying at Reece's place? We could go home?" Harper asked.

Hailey shrugged. "I know you want to be with Nick, and I also know that you wouldn't let me stay home by myself. I'm okay where I'm at for now."

It was true. The thought of going back home and not being with Nick caused pain in her gut and heart. Still, she missed being with Hailey. Missed the sister time they had each night.

"Why don't you come over tonight for dinner? Nick is a wonderful cook. You can see Lucy and Blue."

Hailey glanced around. "I asked for a double shift. I won't get off work until eleven."

"Tomorrow?" Harper asked.

Hailey nodded. "If I can swing it. I'll text you." She glanced at her watch. "I'd better get back to work."

The high of buying the pretty outfit for Friday night had been tempered by her conversation with her sister. There was something between them that had never been there before. Distance.

For all of her life, she and Hailey had been close. So close that it felt like their hearts beat in rhythm. Now, because of her relationship with Nick, she thought that Hailey was pulling away from her. And she didn't think she could bear it.

Still, it hurt just as bad thinking about breaking things off with Nick as it did missing her sister.

By the time she got off work, she had worked herself into an intense headache, something she'd never had before.

Since Nick wasn't home yet, she took both dogs and headed to the beach to clear her head.

While Lucy was used to being on a leash for their walks through the trees that surrounded the cabin, Blue yanked on the leash, trying to get to the beach faster so she could release him.

The narrow pathway that went from Nick's back gate to the opening of the beach went past three other backyards. Tall fences lined the pebble-covered pathway.

Before the path emptied onto the beach, it passed a back road that normally had no cars on it. Today, however, a cargo van sat at the dead-end near the entrance to the park, half a block away.

Harper wondered briefly about the vehicle, but then Blue yanked her arm and pulled her onto the beach.

She removed the dogs' leashes and laughed as they raced towards the water's edge. She followed them and sat in the sand, where she removed her shoes and rolled up her pant legs.

She knew the water would be cold, but the second the waves rushed over her feet and lower legs, she sighed with relief. The sand felt so good between her toes and the water removed the aches from being on her feet all day.

Of course, she could only stand it for a few moments and, once she couldn't feel her toes any longer, she found a nice spot from which to watch the dogs play tug-of-war with a huge stick.

When her phone rang, she answered Nick's call.

"Hi," she answered with a smile, already feeling her headache disappearing.

"Hey, it sounds like you're at the beach?" Nick asked.

"We are. The dogs are fighting over a stick," she said with a chuckle.

Nick was quiet and then said, "I was calling to tell you that I was going to be late. We're heading out on a call halfway to Edgeview."

"Okay." She shifted to hear him better. "Don't worry. When we get back home, I'll have to bathe both dogs and then probably need a shower myself."

"Is it too soon for me to tell you how much hearing you call it home warms me?" Nick said with a slight sigh.

She hadn't noticed that she'd done it, but now she smiled when she realized that his place was just as much a home to her as the cabin was.

"I still think of the cabin as home too," she pointed out.

"Yeah, that's good too," he agreed. "You did only bring a bag of your things over." He muffled the phone while he talked to someone else, presumably Tom. "Hey, I have to go. Call or text me when you get home safely."

"Okay," she said and then hung up.

"Well, well, look who I finally found alone," someone said from directly behind her.

Harper jerked her head around just as a fist slammed into her left temple. Everything spun several times before going black.

She felt the soft sand under her body turn into wet and cold sand. When her body hit the icy water, her mind cleared as two strong hands held her head under the rolling surf.

She gasped, fought for air, only to take in mouthful after

mouthful of salty water. Her nails scratched skin, clothing, anything to try and find release.

She tried to get a glimpse of who it was but could only see the darkness of the water whenever a wave hit her. The only sound was the pounding in her head mixed with the roaring waves pelting her.

Then, clear as day, she heard a man scream in pain, and she was released. She heard the dogs barking and growling, then she heard more screaming. One of dogs yelped in pain.

She fought the current to get on her hands and knees as she gulped air into her sore lungs. Coughing, she panicked as she looked around.

Both dogs were gone. The man was gone.

Had it been Fred? She couldn't tell. His voice sounded... deeper than she remembered.

Pulling herself out of the water took all of her strength. It wasn't until she was lying in the dry sand that her body started to shiver uncontrollably, and she thought to call for help.

She looked around. She knew she'd had her cell phone in her hands when she'd been hit. Double checking, she confirmed it wasn't in her pockets and glanced around the now dark beach.

How long had she been out? How long had she been in the water? Too long. Her body screamed that it was too cold.

She saw a dark blob racing towards her and relaxed when both dogs appeared by her side.

She half crawled with them across the beach and was about to just head back to Nick's place to call for help when she heard her cell phone several yards across the beach. It's screen lighting up was like a beacon in the night.

She fell several times racing towards the spot. Her head

was swimming, and she was so cold she could feel her entire body shutting down. Finally, she made it to the phone and with shaky fingers, swiped the screen to answer Nick's third call.

"Harper?" Nick said before she could say anything into the phone.

"Help," she managed to whisper just before blacking out.

Chapter Twenty

Too long. Everything was taking far too long. Tom jerked the wheel around as he put on the lights while they raced back towards Pride.

The call they'd been going out on would just have to wait. Harper was far more important than a call about a possible dead deer in the road.

Minutes seemed to stretch into hours as he kept screaming Harper's name into the phone.

"Get someone out there now," he told Tom. "Whoever is available. The beach near my place. She's not responding."

Tom nodded and called it in while he listened to the phone. He could hear Blue and Lucy whine and shuffle around. At least they were there.

Whatever had happened to Harper, they were there for her until he could be.

"David and Simon are two blocks away and heading there now," Tom told him.

Shit. They were almost ten minutes away. Ten long fucking minutes. They stretched even longer as he worried.

When Tom finally stopped at the small park's parking area, David and Simon's patrol car was sitting there with the spotlights lighting up the pathway and as much beach as they could.

The second Nick stepped out of the car, he whistled for the dogs as he ran down the pathway.

When they barked, he raced across the sand to were David knelt beside Harper while Simon held onto the dogs.

"She's soaking wet and freezing. We were just about to move her but look," David said, motioning towards Harper's head. A large gash ran from just above her left ear to her temple. "We're thinking we should wait for emergency to get here."

Nick was kneeling beside her now and felt her freezing skin for himself. Without waiting, he picked her up and started racing back down the beach.

"Nick?" Simon called after him.

"I'm taking her myself," he called back.

"Whoever attacked her got your dog."

Nick stopped running and turned around. "Shit, is he okay?" Worry for his dog now mixed with worry for Harper.

"I'll take him to the vet. Go," Simon called. "I've got them. Take care of Harper."

He met Tom halfway back to the parking area. The two raced towards the patrol car just as Harper woke up.

"Nick?" Her arms wrapped around him tightly. "Stop." She groaned.

When he did, she jerked away from him and threw up. Missing his shoes and herself.

"Take me home," she groaned when she was done. "I'm cold." He felt her entire body shivering.

She was soaking wet, getting his clothes wet as well.

Still, he didn't care. However cold it was making him, he knew she was colder.

"You need a doctor," he said, firmly.

"No, just... I want to go home." She cried and laid her head against his chest.

Nick looked at Tom, who just shrugged. At that moment, Simon and Dave came down the beach with the dogs.

"We found their leashes and Harper's phone." Simon held the phone towards him.

Harper held her hand out without looking.

Tom grabbed the phone for her. "Come on, I'll drive you back to your place," he said to them.

"Want me to take Blue to the vet?" Simon asked.

Nick nodded. "How's Lucy?"

"We checked her over, she appears to be okay. The blood, we think, is from whoever attacked Harper."

"Blood?" Harper jerked in his arms. "Are the dogs, okay?"

"Shhh." He held her still. "Let's get you warm first." He nodded to Tom, who took Lucy's leash while Simon and Dave led Blue towards their patrol cars.

He climbed into the car and pulled Harper onto his lap while Lucy sat in the back.

It was less than a block to his house, and the inside of the patrol car was warm.

Tom parked in the drive next to Harper's car. Nick carried Harper inside as Tom followed with Lucy in tow.

"You can put her in the laundry room. I'm taking Harper upstairs to get these wet clothes off and put her in a hot shower," he told Tom.

"Want me to call and see if Dr. Stevens can come over?" Tom asked, leading Lucy back towards the laundry room.

"Sure, but in half an hour. I want to get Harper warmed first." He took two stairs at a time.

"Blue? Is he okay?" Harper asked in a weak voice.

"I don't know. He looked okay when I saw him. Simon and Dave said he had been cut." He set her on the bathroom counter, flipped on the hot water, and then started pulling off her soaking wet clothes. "Want to tell me what happened?" he asked, running his eyes over her while he untied her shoelaces.

Removing her soaked frozen jeans took a lot more effort. She had removed her shirt herself and waited while he worked to get her pants off.

The gash just above her left ear wasn't as bad as it had looked on the beach. Actually, when he used the clean towel to wipe away the blood, there was only a small cut near her temple. The rest was bruised.

"He hit me the second I got off the phone with you," she said.

"Was it Fred?" he asked as she stood up and tossed off her undergarments.

When she wobbled on her feet, he reached for her and helped her into the shower, where she sat down and leaned into the hot water.

"I don't know. Honestly, I didn't see him. It happened so fast. When he hit me, I blacked out. I came to when he put me in the water. Then, he..." He heard her voice change. She gasped and then pulled her knees up to her chest and buried her face into them. "He tried to drown me," she said softly. "I... I can't swim. I panicked. God." She cried and he wished more than anything he could jump in there and hold her.

Shit. Nick wanted to go after the guy.

Then she jerked up and looked at him with complete fear in her eyes. "Hailey," she said, her skin pale white.

Understanding her, he pulled out his cell phone and called her sister.

Hailey answered on the second ring. Instantly, he could tell she was either at work or in another public place.

"Where are you?" he asked her.

"Work," Hailey answered. "Why?"

"Stay put. I'm having Reece head your way," Nick said.

"He's already here. What's happened?" Hailey asked, her tone sounding scared.

"Someone attacked Harper on the beach. She's okay, but they tried to drown her. She's warming up before the doctor gets here to look her over."

"We're heading over there," Hailey said before hanging up.

"She's with Reece." He watched her relax and lay her head back down. "They're heading over here now. How are you doing?" he asked, wishing he could join her. Instead, he pulled off his uniform and changed into his own clothes while keeping an eye on Harper.

When she reached up and shut off the water, he had a towel and her bathrobe waiting for her.

"Want sweats and a sweatshirt?" he asked her.

She nodded as she buried herself in the robe and wrapped her long hair in the towel. "You're still bleeding." He motioned towards her head and then lifted her to sit on the countertop so he could clean and bandage the small cut.

Then he pulled out the army sweats she had borrowed that first night she'd slept over. It hadn't been that long since that first night and yet so much had changed.

"Feeling better?" he asked after she pulled them on and was trying to comb through her hair.

"I'm sort of sick, uneasy stomach," she said with a slight groan.

"A bump on the head will do that," he assured her.

"Yeah, I know." She brushed her teeth. "Maybe some bread or toast?"

He pulled her into his arms. "You don't think..." He held his breath as she melted in his arms.

"No, I'm not pregnant," she said into his chest. "I... got a test at the store and checked."

He closed his eyes and silently wished she was.

Just then his doorbell rang. He heard Tom answer it.

"Sounds like your sister is here." He kissed the top of her head. "I'll show her up and make you something light to eat."

He met Hailey at the bottom of the stairs. "Last door on the right," he told her. "She just got out of the shower and is dressed," he said as she passed him.

He shook Reece's hand.

"Want to fill me in?" Reece asked as Lucy rushed to sniff Reece.

Obviously, Tom had taken the time to clean the blood off the dog's fur.

"Simon called from the vet while you were upstairs," Tom said, holding up his phone. "Blue has a cut on his ear. Nicked a chunk of it off. The vet seems to think he was kicked pretty bad. She's keeping him overnight."

Amelia Brogan, Aiden's mother, had taken over as head veterinarian for the Pride clinic a few years after Nick had started middle school. His family had trusted her with all of their animals growing up. Everyone in town did. Her daughter, Aiden's sister, Carrie, ran an animal refuge just on the outskirts of town. Carrie's husband, Josh, ran

Internet Security, one of the biggest internet security firms in the state.

"Thanks," he said as he walked into the kitchen.

"I'm going to head out," Tom said, as he glanced down at his phone. "It looks like the deer call was a bust. It was a large trash bag." He shook his head. "Still, Aiden has clocked you out for the next two days and told me to tell you to take care of Harper."

Nick relaxed and then shook his brother-in-law's hand. "Thanks for cleaning up Lucy."

Tom nodded, then slugged Reece on the shoulder playfully and walked out.

"Drink?" he asked Reece when they were alone.

"Sure." He took a seat at the bar top.

"Harper wants some toast," he said and started to make her some.

He grabbed a beer for himself and downed a quarter of it.

"Scared you?" Reece asked.

"Hell yeah, it did." Nick sighed and waited for the toast. "She was freezing. He hit her over the head and then tried to drown her. Who in the hell does that? Why? It's bullshit if it's about some stupid insurance money. The company called me earlier today and said they cancelled the policy years ago."

"So why, then? Why is this guy after them?" Reece asked.

Nick leaned on the counter towards him. "What has Hailey told you?"

Reece shrugged. "That this guy was dating their mother before she passed. That he was abusive and now he's stalking them."

Nick closed his eyes and took a deep breath. "It's not my story to tell," he said, just as the toast popped up.

He pulled out the Nutella and set it and the toast on a plate. He poured a large glass of orange juice and set a seltzer next to it, then added a handful of grapes on the side. He had just picked up the tray when the doorbell rang.

"That'll be Dr. Stevens. Let him in. I'm taking this up to Harper."

Reece walked over and opened the door as Nick climbed the stairs.

He heard Reece greet Dr. Stevens and knew that Harper would have to agree to see the man before he'd let him upstairs.

He knocked on the closed bedroom door.

"Come in," Hailey answered.

Harper was lying on the bed, her sister sitting beside her.

"I brought you some toast." He set the tray down. "Dr. Stevens is here..."

"I don't need a doctor," Harper said quickly.

"I know, but still, it would make me feel better if he took a look at that." He motioned to the side of her head. "You know, clean it up. In case I missed some dirt or sand."

Hailey took Harper's hand and nodded. "Just let him look you over. For Nick's peace of mind." She smiled at her sister.

Harper nodded. "Fine." She motioned to the food. "Bring that here."

He took the tray and set it on the bed next to her.

She opened the seltzer and took a drink. "Thanks," she said, meeting his eyes.

He turned to Hailey. "How much do you want Reece to know?" he asked her.

Hailey frowned and then crossed her arms over her chest. "I'll tell him everything myself. For now, just... tell him that Fred attacked Harper tonight."

He nodded and then left.

He shook Dr. Aaron Stevens's hand when he met the man at the bottom of the stairs.

"How is she?" Aaron asked.

Nick had been going to Dr. Stevens his entire life. He was not only his doctor, but a close family friend.

"Thanks for coming, Aaron." Nick shook his head. "She's still pale. I cleaned up the gash right here." He ran his finger over where Harper had a cut. "It appears to be small, but still, she says she blacked out, and she threw up when I was carrying her away from the beach. She says she still feels sick to her stomach. I gave her some seltzer and toast."

Aaron nodded. "A bump on the head will do that. Is she up for a visit?"

He nodded. "Head on up. I told her you were coming."

Aaron nodded and then walked up the stairs.

While they waited, Nick turned back to Reece. "I've been instructed that Hailey will fill you in completely. For now, we believe it was Fred who attacked Harper tonight. She didn't get a look at who it was, but we're pretty sure it was him."

Reece's eyes moved to the stairs then he turned back to him. "Why? Why is their mother's old boyfriend going after them?"

Nick took a deep breath. "You'll have to ask Hailey. I'm sorry." He shook his head and felt like punching something.

Chapter Twenty-One

Harper was grateful that Hailey was there when Doctor Stevens walked into the room. She'd never been examined by a doctor before. Neither of them had.

Doctors were something only the rich could afford. And growing up, they had been very far from rich.

Actually, doctors were to be feared as much as the police and social services.

Hailey held her hand while Dr. Stevens, a man she knew and liked, examined her.

Still, she felt uneasy the entire time as he flashed a light in her eyes and checked her head, her ears, her throat. When he pulled out a needle and told her he was going to draw some blood for tests, she almost passed out.

She'd never had blood drawn before. When she'd been a child, her mother had taken her and Hailey to those free clinics to get their vaccines. Never had they drawn blood though.

"I..." She shook her head.

"Easy," Dr. Stevens said with a smile. "I promise, you won't feel a thing. Just keep your eyes on your sister."

Harper nodded and then glued her eyes on Hailey's face.

Her sister's hair had lightened some in the past year. She'd cut it and the style really fit her. Actually, the more she thought about it, the more she realized how much girlier Hailey was than she was.

She jerked when she felt the needle slide into her skin.

"You good?" Dr. Stevens asked.

Harper nodded and ran her eyes over Hailey's. Her sister knew how to do her makeup better than Harper did too. She also dressed more stylishly than she did.

She supposed she'd been so preoccupied with making sure Hailey was okay that she'd put her own life on hold. Nothing had mattered to her except Hailey.

While her sister had grown and thrived, Harper had lived in fear, hiding from everything.

She loved Hailey. Actually, up until she met Nick, Hailey was the only person in the world that she loved.

"There, all done," Dr. Steven said. "Now, I think you're in good hands with Nick. But just to play it safe, you're on bed rest tomorrow. If you continue to feel uneasy"—he patted his stomach—"let me know. You can take some antacids if you need. Tylenol for headaches. If you feel dizzy or things just don't feel right, call me." He stood up to go, then he turned to Hailey. "Now that I've examined your sister, why don't you call my office and set up an appointment too." He walked out.

"He's nice." Hailey sighed. "I suppose we need to stop fearing doctors."

Harper smiled and took her sister's hand in hers. "I love you."

"I love you too," Hailey said.

"I love Nick," Harper said with a smile. "I think... I think I want to move in here. To live with him. But I..." She shook her head as tears filled her eyes. "I don't want to leave you."

Hailey reached over and hugged her. "You won't be leaving me. I'll always be here."

"I won't move in here officially until after Fred is locked up," Harper said against her sister's hair.

Hailey nodded. "I'm staying put until that man is behind bars. Reece says I can stay in his guest room for however long that takes. He's invited me to go with him to Vegas and California next month to see his fight."

Harper leaned back and smiled. "You should go. We liked Vegas, remember?"

Hailey nodded. "Are you okay?" She brushed a strand of Harper's hair away from her face.

Harper nodded and then was shocked when she burst out crying as she relayed everything that had happened to her.

For the next hour, the sisters lay in the bed and talked about their past, something they'd never really done before.

What had happened to them, what both their mother and Fred had done, had been the elephant in the room. Taboo to talk about, even though both of them suffered inside.

At one point Nick showed up and offered to get them something more to eat or drink. Both sisters declined, but then they joked that the conversation needed wine or ice cream.

Harper felt a million pounds lighter after saying the words she'd felt inside all of these years. She told Hailey that she loved her and would give up her life for her, but that she'd felt it was her duty to protect her above all else, above living her own life.

Hailey opened up to Harper about how she'd felt guilty that she couldn't take care of herself.

"I never knew what Fred was doing to you. Not until after that night," Hailey confessed.

"You were young. No one ever talked to us about those sorts of things," Harper said.

Hailey shook her head. "How, how can you be with Nick now and not"—tears rolled down Hailey's cheeks—"and not think back?"

Harper hugged Hailey, closing her eyes tight.

"It's different. Sex with someone you like or love is magical. It's like night and day." She wished more than anything for better words to explain the differences. "Do you like Reece?" Hailey nodded. "Have you kissed yet?" Hailey nodded again. "How did it feel?"

Hailey was quiet for a moment. "Magical."

Harper smiled and leaned back, brushing a strand of her sister's hair from her eyes. "Trust him. Trust yourself. The rest will be just as special."

Hailey rolled her eyes. "It's sort of embarrassing."

"Life is embarrassing if you make it. Embrace yourself, sex, Reece, whatever comes next. Being with Nick has opened my eyes to all that was taken from us. The more I'm with him, the more I realize just how much we lost. And at this point, I want it all." She smiled. "Everything I never knew to dream about."

Hailey hugged her. "I love you."

"I love you." Harper laughed as tears rolled down both of their cheeks.

The next time Nick knocked on the door, Reece and

Lucy were with him. Lucy, who normally never jumped up on the bed, rushed to Harper's side.

"Just this once," Harper said, snuggling the dog to her side.

"How are you feeling?" Reece asked her, but his eyes moved to Hailey's face, which was red from crying, much like Harper's.

"Great." She squeezed Hailey's hand. "Just girl talk." She nodded and her sister hugged her once more before getting off the bed.

Nick moved to take the spot. "Everything okay?"

"Yeah." She nodded to him. "I think I could rest now." She felt drained after the emotional evening.

"We'll head out," Hailey said, standing next to Reece. "If you need anything..."

"Thanks for taking care of my sister," Harper said to Reece. "If you hurt her, I'll slap on my boxing gloves and kick your butt."

Reece smiled and nodded. Then he wrapped an arm around Hailey's shoulders and walked out.

"They're going to be okay," she said out loud.

"Course they are," Nick agreed. "Reece is like a brother to me." He pulled her into a light hug. "How's the head?"

"Fine. Dull pain is all. I think talking to Hailey was the best medicine."

"I figured you'd need some time with her."

"Thanks." Harper held in a yawn.

"Want anything?"

"Ice cream." She sighed and snuggled back down.

"I'll be right back." He shifted to get off the bed.

"How's Blue?" she asked.

He stopped and smiled. "He got a few stitches, but I can pick him up in the morning."

She shook her head. "I think they saved my life tonight."

Nick's smile fell as he nodded. "Yeah." His eyes moved over to Lucy, who was snoring while half of her body covered Harper's. "Yeah," he agreed again and turned and walked out.

Harper lay there, running her fingers through Lucy's thick fur and musing about just how lucky she'd gotten in the past few months.

After a bowl of Rocky Road covered with chocolate syrup, crushed pecans, and Cool Whip, she fell into a deep sleep filled with dreams of puppies and children playing together.

When she woke, Nick was already out of bed. She could hear him on the phone in the bathroom and strained to hear what he was saying.

Something about a hospital.

When he ended the call and stepped back into the room, he smiled at her.

"Who was that?" she asked.

"Tom. A man matching Fred's description was at the Edgeview hospital last night. He claimed that a stray dog bit him. He received thirteen stitches on his arms and suffered a broken finger." While Nick said this, he smiled, then it dropped. "They released him after patching him up."

"So it was him." In her heart, she'd known it was. Even if she hadn't seen him.

"Yeah, we've put out a statewide search for him." Nick sat next to her. He was quiet for a moment then smiled. "How about some French toast in bed?"

She smiled and nodded. "The kind you made with bananas and caramel syrup?" she asked.

"Bananas Foster?" He nodded. "Coming right up. You stay in bed."

"Bathroom first." She pulled the covers off her legs.

Nick gasped and rushed to her side.

Both of her legs were covered with bruises and tiny scratches from the sand and rocks.

"It looks worse than it feels," she told him as he ran his fingers gently over her legs.

"We should put something on these. Did Dr. Stevens see these?"

She nodded. "He told me I could put some of that on the worst of them." She motioned to the tube he'd given her the night before.

Nick nodded. "Can I help?"

She shook her head. "No, you go make me breakfast. I'll clean up and take care of this." She took the tube from him, then kissed him. "I'm hungry."

He chuckled and bowed slightly. "Your wish is my command."

She laughed and nudged him aside, then stood up and wobbled towards the bathroom. She tried desperately not to, but her legs were shaky.

She tied her hair up in a bun and warmed herself up under the hot shower spray while trying to keep her hair dry.

After applying some of the goo that Dr. Stevens had given her to the worst cuts on her legs, she put a few bandages over them and pulled on another pair of Nick's sweats and one of his army T-shirts.

When she returned to bed, Nick was there with her breakfast on a tray.

They sat in the bed together, eating the meal and talking about her conversation with her sister.

She told him everything. For once in her life, she didn't

hold anything back, much like the conversation she'd had with Hailey the night before.

It felt good. It felt right.

She felt complete.

After breakfast, she watched some television and then napped.

By midday, she was bored and so ready for a walk. Lucy was whining and obviously missing Blue.

Hailey and Reece showed up just before lunch with a pizza. Nick took that time to run to get Blue from the vet.

When he came back, he informed her that the vet had also neutered Blue while he was there. Blue did not look happy. He had a cone around his head so he wouldn't bother the stitches on his ear and private parts.

Harper held the dog to her side and thanked him for saving her. There was a small chunk missing from his right ear.

All in all, the dog had weathered the storm worse than she had. Still, after seeing her, Blue became bouncy and full of life again.

"They need a walk," Nick said after Reece and Hailey left.

"I want one too." She stood to put on her shoes and jacket.

She watched Nick open his mouth to argue, but then he sighed and nodded. "A short one."

"We can take them to the beach," she said. "Then I can sit and watch them run."

Nick nodded and helped her slip on her coat.

They walked hand in hand, Nick holding the leashes in his other hand.

Harper noticed Blue didn't tug as much as he had the day before.

When they passed the street area before the beach, she stilled.

"The van," she whispered, remembering the white cargo van.

"What?" Nick asked, turning towards her.

"There was a white cargo van parked there yesterday when we passed by." She motioned to the spot. "It had to be him."

"White cargo van." Nick nodded. "Any other details you can tell me? If it was him, we can keep an eye out for it."

She thought back. "It had a worn sticker in the back right window. There was a dent in the left back side." She shrugged. "Maybe out-of-state plates?" She shrugged. "They were orange looking."

Nick nodded and pulled out his phone after they stepped onto the beach and he'd unhooked the dogs. While he called and relayed this information to Tom, the dogs raced to the water and down the beach to find a stick.

Harper sat in the sand while Nick paced and talked on the phone.

When he was done, he sat next to her.

"They're pulling the video from the hospital's parking lot to confirm the vehicle," he told her as he took her hand.

They sat in silence for a few moments before she turned to him.

"I'm going to move in with you," she said with a smile.

Nick smiled and then hugged her.

"Officially, after you catch Fred," she added. Nick nodded in agreement. "When I know that Hailey is safe."

Nick leaned back, his eyes running over hers. She could see the excitement and happiness in his eyes.

"I'll take it. You're staying put though, here with us, until then?"

She shrugged. "If Hailey wants to return home, I'll go with her until he's caught." Nick opened his mouth to argue, but she added, "You don't get a say in that."

He took a deep breath and nodded. "Fine."

"There's one more thing," She turned fully towards him. "I love you. I've never said that to anyone."

"I love you too," he burst out, and then kissed her. "God, I was going to tell you on Valentine's Day. I had this whole thing planned." He sighed.

She chuckled. "I'm sorry if I ruined it."

He shook his head. "No, you didn't." He leaned back again. "I love you. I can say it as many times as I want."

She smiled. "I love you."

They laughed and hugged again just as the wet dogs attacked them and tried to join in the fun.

Epilogue

Harper tugged on the short skirt of the pretty dress as she looked at herself in the mirror one last time. It had taken most of her makeup to hide all the cuts and bruises on her legs but it was worth it.

Hailey had helped her curl her hair earlier that day and, thankfully, some of the curls had stayed.

Since it was a gray day outside, she pulled the cream-colored sweater over the dress before heading down the stairs.

Nick stood at the bottom of the steps in khakis and a dress shirt. He looked so handsome. Both of the dogs were sitting at his feet as the trio watched her.

"Wow," Nick said under his breath. "You look so amazing," he said when she stopped on the last step. He walked over and brushed his lips across hers.

Then he held up a small box. "I figured I'd get your first gift out of the way since you already gave me mine." He motioned to the photo of the buck hanging over the fireplace that she'd given him earlier that morning. She'd replaced the old photo with this one when he'd been in the shower.

She smiled and took the box from him.

"Open it," he suggested.

She did and smiled. Inside was a set of keys to the house and two dog tags. The dog tags had their names along with the address on them. Nick's address. Their address.

"The keys to my heart and my home," Nick said with a smile.

She hugged him.

"Ready?" he asked after they took the time to put the new dog tags on both the dogs' collars.

"Ready." She stepped out with him.

They rode in the Jeep to the Golden Oar, but instead of heading into the restaurant, they walked down to the small dock near it instead.

There, at the base of the dock, a candlelight dinner was set up for them.

"Wow," she gasped when she saw the romantic scene. "I didn't know the restaurant offered this." She laughed as he held out a chair for her.

"They don't normally, but for you they made an exception." He winked as he sat down next to her.

Jordan, one of the waitstaff, appeared with a tray of food while Nick opened the bottle of champagne and poured them each a glass.

While they ate, they talked about her move into his place. About the dogs. About the view.

When they had finished enjoying their meal of braised salmon over wild rice and vegetables, he took her hand and walked towards the end of the dock.

"I have one more gift for you," he said as he turned to her.

"I have one for you too." She smiled.

His eyebrows shot up in question. "You go first."

She nodded and then took a deep breath.

"I had a call from Dr. Stevens this morning." Nick waited for her to continue. "It appears that the test that I took wasn't very accurate."

He frowned. "Test?"

She waited until her meaning dawned on him. The sheer excitement in his face meant so much to her.

"You mean...? Say it." His hand tightened slightly on hers.

She laughed. "I'm pregnant."

He let out a loud whoop sound and then pulled her into a hug and spun her around several times.

"I take it that you're happy about this?" she laughed.

"Who wouldn't be?" He smiled. "Which brings me to my present." He released her suddenly and then, to her surprise, dropped down on one knee and pulled out a small black box.

"Harper Davis, will you marry me? I had a bunch of other things I wanted to say, but I'm too excited right now to remember them all. I swear though that if you say yes, I'll spend a lifetime thinking of wonderful things to say to you." The words burst from Nick in one long string of excitement.

She laughed and then took the ring out of the box and slid it on her finger. "Yes, I'll take it and you. Just as long as you continue to love me."

He jumped up and hugged her again. "Always, my love," he whispered just before he kissed her.

Also by Jill Sanders

The Pride Series

Finding Pride

Discovering Pride

Returning Pride

Lasting Pride

Serving Pride

Red Hot Christmas

My Sweet Valentine

Return To Me

Rescue Me

A Pride Christmas

The Secret Series

Secret Seduction

Secret Pleasure

Secret Guardian

Secret Passions

Secret Identity

Secret Sauce

Secret Obsession

Secret Desire

Secret Charm

Secret Santa

The West Series

Loving Lauren

Taming Alex

Holding Haley

Missy's Moment

Breaking Travis

Roping Ryan

Wild Bride

Corey's Catch

Tessa's Turn

Saving Trace

Christmas Holly

Maggie's Match

The Grayton Series

Last Resort

Someday Beach

Rip Current

In Too Deep

Swept Away

High Tide

Sunset Dreams

Lucky Series

Unlucky In Love

Sweet Resolve

Best of Luck

A Little Luck

Christmas Wish

Silver Cove Series

Silver Lining

French Kiss

Happy Accident

Hidden Charm

A Silver Cove Christmas

Sweet Surrender

Second Chances

Dancing on Air

Entangled Series – Paranormal Romance

The Awakening

The Beckoning

The Ascension

The Presence

The Calling

The Chosen

The Beyond

The Void

Haven, Montana Series

Closer to You

Never Let Go
Holding On
Coming Home
The Hard Way
Never Again

Pride Oregon Series

A Dash of Love
My Kind of Love
Season of Love
Tis the Season
Dare to Love
Where I Belong
Because of Love
A Thing Called Love
First Comes Love
Someone to Love
Fools in Love
FindingLove
Christmas Joy
Always My Love
Forever My Love
Searching for Love

Wildflowers Series

Summer Nights
Summer Heat

Summer Secrets
Summer Fling
Summer's End
Summer Wish
Summer Breeze
Summer Ride

Distracted Series
Wake Me
Tame Me
Save Me
Dare Me

Stand Alone Books
Twisted Rock
Hope Harbor
Raven Falls
Angel Bluff
Day Break
Diamonds in the Mud

For a complete list of books:
http://JillSanders.com

About the Author

Jill Sanders is a New York Times, USA Today, and international bestselling author of Sweet Contemporary Romance, Romantic Suspense, Western Romance, and Paranormal Romance novels. With over 90 books in eleven series, translations into several different languages, and audiobooks there's plenty to choose from. Look for Jill's bestselling stories wherever romance books are sold or visit her at jillsanders.com

Jill comes from a large family with six siblings, including an identical twin. She was raised in the Pacific Northwest and later relocated to Colorado for college and a successful IT career before discovering her talent for writing sweet and sexy page-turners. After Colorado, she decided to move south, living in Texas and now making her home along the Emerald Coast of Florida. You will find that the settings of several of her series are inspired by her time spent living in these areas. She has two sons and off-set the testosterone in her house by adopting three furry little ladies that provide her company while she's locked in her writing cave. She enjoys heading to the beach, hiking, swimming, wine-tasting, and pickleball with her husband, and of course writing. If you have read any of her books, you may also notice that there is a love of food, especially sweets! She has been blamed for a few added pounds by her assistant, editor, and fans... donuts or pie anyone?

- facebook.com/JillSandersBooks
- x.com/JillMSanders
- amazon.com/Jill-Sanders/e/B009M2NFD6?tag=jillm-com-20
- bookbub.com/authors/jill-sanders
- instagram.com/jillsandersauthor
- tiktok.com/@jillsandersauthor

www.ingramcontent.com/pod-product-compliance
Lightning Source LLC
LaVergne TN
LVHW041805060526
838201LV00046B/1131